DYSTOPIA

Janet McNulty

This is a work of fiction. The names, characters, places, and incidents within are the product of the author's imagination or are used fictitiously, and any resemblance to actual persons, living or dead, business establishments, events, or location is entirely coincidental. The publisher does not have any control over and does not assume any responsibility for author or third-party websites or their content.

Dystopia

ISBN-10: 0615762581 (MMP Publishing)
ISBN-13: 978-0615762586

Printed in the United States of America

~ To all of the Dana Ginary's in the world

DYSTOPIA

CHAPTER ONE

Dana dumped the open suitcase on the bed and piled clothes inside it. She and her sister, Lina, raced through the room, cramming what they could into the medium sized, brown grip.

"Hurry!" their father yelled from the bottom of the stairs.

Banging resounded downstairs as gloved fists pounded the front door.

Dana snapped the suitcase closed and handed it to her sister. Just as they reached the door to the hallway, uniformed officers burst into their room knocking her to the floor. The suitcase flew across the space and crashed into the far wall, opening and spilling its contents.

An iron fist gripped Dana's forearm and scanned the chip implanted in it. Another scanned Lina's. "Her," he said, pointing to Dana's sister.

Armed men seized Lina and dragged her out of the

room amidst the screams and shouts of the family. Dana lunged for her sister. One of the officers thrust her aside. She banged her head on the table and collapsed to the floor unconscious, as her sister kicked and screamed.

Dana woke up. Sweat covered her skin, making her pajamas and blanket cling to her. Slowly, she realized that she had been dreaming and over five years had passed since her sister was taken for failure to report to Wing 16 of the Hospital.

Dana glanced at the empty bed in the room, her sister's bed. Dawn poked through the curtains.

Screams echoed from outside. Carefully, Dana looked out her window, and across the way, she watched as armed officers entered her neighbor's house. They hauled out a man who struggled profusely to get away. His wife screamed and cried as she pleaded for them to let him go. *No wonder I had the dream.*

"Don't get involved," she repeated to herself.

"Dana, you're going to be late," her mother called from the bottom of the stairs.

She glanced at her clock and realized that once again she was late for school and this was career assignment day. Quickly, Dana tossed off the covers and threw on some clothes. She darted down the stairs. She paused when she passed the living room. The television was tuned into the only government approved talk show with Mr. Halloway.

He smiled that charismatic smile of his as he interviewed the First Councilman of the western region: Donald Humphries. Dana listened momentarily as they talked about the resistance.

"Dana."

"Sorry, mom." Dana ran out the door after giving her mother a kiss. No time for breakfast.

Dana briefly stopped and glanced at her neighbor's house as the man was shoved inside a van. One of the officers glanced in her direction. Hurriedly, she looked away and walked toward the bus stop for the first bus into the city.

She stared at her lap the entire ride, sinking into her seat. *No need to draw attention.* Two officers sat in the row in front of her. Dana's pulse throbbed like it always did when she came into contact with them. The least infraction meant being arrested, or worse. She fiddled with her fingers as she anxiously awaited her stop.

The bus lurched. Dana's already nauseous stomach did a whirl as it threatened to upchuck on her. When her stop neared, she pressed the button and jumped off, relieved to be out of its confined atmosphere.

Dana raced through the pristine streets of the city, her feet pounding on the marbled sidewalks. She scrambled up a bunch of stairs. *Late again!* Ignoring the pain in her side, Dana ran faster as she headed to the school, her jet black hair billowing behind her.

It was graduation day and she had woken up late. Graduation day meant the day when you received your career assignment. Most looked forward to it. Dana dreaded it. At the age of 17, students graduated from school. No ceremony marked the event, just a letter from the Career Assignment Board telling you what you would do for the rest of your life.

Dana increased her speed. Tardiness was frowned upon. Not a good way to make a good impression, she thought.

The arched doorway to the school loomed ahead. Dana charged through the glass doors as she darted past the man at the desk.

"Hey, you need to sign…"

"No time," said Dana as she dashed down the hallway.

She found the door to her classroom. Peeking through the window, Dana saw her teacher, Bill Torres, handing out crisp, white envelopes.

"Shoot," whispered Dana to herself.

When her teacher turned his back, Dana quietly opened the heavy door and slipped inside. She headed straight for her desk and sat down.

"You're late," hissed Kenny.

Dana glared at him.

Kenny Michaels was one of her school friends who had a knack for pointing out the obvious.

"Did you forget what day it was?"

"Shush," Dana hissed at Kenny.

"Miss Ginary," said Bill Torres as he handed Dana her envelope, "Nice of you to join us."

Dana gave a wry smile as she took the envelope. Carefully, she broke the seal and pulled out the letter. Dreading what it would say, she unfolded it, taking note of the seal on the top.

Waste Management.

Dana slapped the paper face down on her desk. *Waste Management?* Had she been that troublesome?

Dana remembered hearing about how a boy received the same assignment two years previously. He was dead three months later. Waste Management was where they sent those they deemed too bothersome, but could not execute outright. The life expectancy there was short-lived.

She knew that she tended to ask a lot of questions and do things her way, but Dana never thought it would lead to this.

"What'd you get?" Kenny snatched the paper from Dana before she could react. "I got Ministry. It will—Oh." He handed her back the letter. "I told you to quit causing so much trouble. I bet that incident in the kitchens was the last straw."

Dana frowned. She remembered the event. Six months ago, she had discovered a book about frying food, something that was forbidden by the council. The council was a group of five men who supposedly made the rules. In reality, they just said yes to whatever the president wanted.

After discovering the book, Dana snuck down to the kitchens in the school with a group of students. She heated up a big pot of oil and fried chicken, bread, and anything else she could think of. They all enjoyed the food and had such a good time that they forgot they were doing something illegal.

Eventually, a bunch of officers showed up and arrested them. Since they were all still considered minors, they were let go with a warning. But Dana knew that she had been singled out as the instigator. She remembered sitting before the principal as he explained to her the errors of her ways. After vowing to never do it again, he let her go with a warning, the latest of many.

"Are there any questions?"

Bill Torres' voice broke through Dana's musings. She raised her hand. The room fell eerily silent as all eyes turned toward her.

"Miss Ginary? Something wrong?"

"I want to change my assignment."

Gasps rippled across the room. No one ever requested a career change.

"A change?"

"Yes," answered Dana. "It is allowed."

"If there is nothing else," said Mr. Torres, "you are all dismissed. Miss Ginary, a word."

Kenny glanced at Dana as he left. Dana walked up to the desk where her teacher sat.

"You do realize how highly irregular this is."

"Yes," replied Dana.

"And you are certain you wish to go through with it?"

"Yes."

"Dana, don't do it."

Dana could not believe what she was hearing. Mr. Torres giving her advice?

"Your record is a huge red flag," said Mr. Torres. "You have been marked repeatedly for being challenging, inquisitive, anti-social, and the incident in the kitchens six months ago was it."

Dana hung her head. It seemed as though she could do nothing right. She knew she shouldn't, but she always questioned what people in authority told her. She tended to prefer working alone instead of in a group. Too independent, people had accused her of.

"Take my advice," continued her teacher. "Take your assignment. It has happened before where a person was able to achieve a different career after working their first assignment for a couple of years. Consider this penance. Don't challenge the council on this."

"That is assuming I live that long. You know the life expectancy for someone in Waste Management. I want to request an assignment change. I may not get another chance."

Reluctantly, Bill Torres pulled out a slip of paper. "Sign here."

Dana put her name on the line.

Mr. Torres attached the slip to her letter and sealed it in another envelope. "I wish you luck."

Dana nodded and left the room. Once outside, she breathed deeply, glad to be out of the confines of the classroom. Dana took one last look at the school, knowing she would never return. Tomorrow, she was to start her assignment.

"So," said Kenny as he ran up to her. He had waited for her to come out.

"I signed the request form," said Dana.

"You what?" Kenny gawked at her in disbelief. "No one does that. You should just take your assignment."

"Says the man who was assigned to the ministry. Did your father pull some strings for that?"

"Hey!"

Dana regretted her statement. She liked Kenny and thought him a good friend, but he never questioned anything. He always just accepted what the council told them. Everyone knew that his father was the First Councilman of the eastern region and had some influence to garner extra luxuries for his family, luxuries denied to everyone else.

"Sorry," said Dana.

"Hey, you two!" Emily Melk ran up to them. "We got it! We got it!"

"Got what, Em?" asked Dana.

"John and I will be allowed to live together. The permit just came through today."

Emily waved the official slip of paper in front of them.

"Congratulations," said Kenny.

"We're thinking of applying for a child next," said Emily with excitement.

"I don't see why you need a permit for anything," muttered Dana.

"See, that's what I mean," Kenny turned on her. "You always question things. Don't you realize that all this is necessary so that no one has opportunities denied to another?"

Dana bit back her retort. "Sorry. Congrats, Emily. I know you've been looking forward to this."

"So you guys got your assignments today?" Emily had graduated a year before and worked in Food Management, which meant she worked in one of the many grocery stores. It wasn't a bad job. Usually, it meant that the person got some extra treats, as many within Food Management would sneak away with canned goods, figuring that they were owed them.

"Yes," said Kenny. "I get to work in the Ministry."

"Oh, that's a good place. Lots of room for advancement." Emily turned to Dana.

"I need to be going," said Dana, not wanting to talk about her assignment. "I'll see you two later, but I need to get some milk before I return home."

She ran off and caught the next bus that would take her to the market closest to her home. As the bus bounced down the street, Dana watched as the marbled buildings of downtown disappeared, being replaced by more shabby looking ones. They passed a green area where those selected to be officers trained. Sunlight glistened off their bare skin.

Dana got off at her stop and headed straight for the grocer, taking special care to avoid the officers that patrolled the streets. She took her place in line once she entered the market building.

"Next."

Dana rushed to the counter. "One gallon of milk, please."

The man behind the counter disappeared and came back a few minutes later with a half-gallon.

"I asked for a gallon," said Dana.

"Doesn't matter," said the man. "New regulations. Now each family gets just a half-gallon of milk for the week."

"But..."

"If you don't want it, then just leave."

Dana took the milk. The man grabbed her arm and scanned the chip that was implanted in her forearm. She watched as a spot of red appeared and vanished.

Upon birth, each person received a chip that was implanted in their arm. The chip revealed everything about you to anyone with a scanner. It also served as a tracking device.

Dana took her milk and left.

"Next!"

To her dismay, Dana noticed that not only had the quantity changed, but it was 1% instead of 2%.

"I wish they would quit changing the rules," said one man to a few others.

"What was that?" demanded one. "Are you disagreeing with the president and therefore disagreeing with society?"

"No, I just..."

The man who had muttered discontent soon found himself on the pavement as the others beat him. Dana watched for a moment. When one of the others looked at her, she ran away. An officer strolled by, ignoring the entire affair. Disagreement was a punishable offense.

Dana turned a corner. She raced down the alley toward the street that led to her home. Within 15 minutes, she entered her neighborhood. Somberly, Dana observed the "cookie cutter" houses and how they looked exactly the same. Each house possessed the same square footage and a quarter acre of land. This prevented anyone from having more than someone else.

A vacant house caught her attention. Pausing, Dana remembered the man who used to live there. He had turned one of the rooms into a greenhouse and sold the produce to supplement his income. But someone had informed the Officer Corps. Dana remembered the raid that took place as officers dragged the man from his home and placed a black bag over his head. They ransacked the building, destroying the plants he had managed to grow. Once things had quieted down, Dana snuck inside and salvaged what she could. She never told her mother where the extra produce came from.

Realizing it grew late, Dana hurried to her house. She pulled the mail out of the box and went inside.

"Dana?" Her mother stepped out of the kitchen. "You're late. Wash up. Supper will be ready soon."

Dana put the milk away and handed her father the mail. He took one letter and tossed the rest aside. "Hmmph! Seems we get less and less each time."

Dana glanced at what her father referred to. He had opened up the envelope with his paycheck. Each pay period, a person's paycheck was sent to the treasury. There the government took what they deemed necessary as taxes and to pay the individual's bills. What was left over was what the individual person was allowed to keep, his allotment.

"Well, Dana is leaving us now," said her mother. "Seventeen and starting her own career." Her mother gave her a tearful look. "Well, time enough for that. Supper's ready."

The electricity shut off.

"Oh, dear," said her mother, "did we go through our

allotment again?" She lit a lamp and set it on the table. "Sometimes I think they keep lessening how much we can use."

"It's all about saving the environment, dear," muttered Dana's father.

"Shh," warned her mother. "Don't say such things so loud."

Dana took her seat as her mother placed a plate in front of her. The plate contained only a half cup of rice, a full cup of peas, and one piece of chicken. Because people received government-provided health care, the government decided that they had to manage what people ate. Officially, it was done for health reasons and national security. In reality, they did it because resources were limited and costs needed to be kept down.

Her father pushed his chicken onto her plate, putting a finger over his mouth. "Don't tell your mother."

Dana smiled and ate it quickly.

A knock sounded at the door. Jumping up, Dana ran to the door and yanked it open. A letter stuck out of the mailbox. She took it, knowing what it was. With shaking fingers, she opened it.

Request Denied.

"Dana, what was it?" Her mother walked into the hallway, taking the letter before Dana could hide it. A frown appeared on her face. "You tried to change your career assignment?"

"They put me in Waste Management. I just wanted…"

Dana stopped when she noticed her mother turn white.

"It's okay, mom. I will work there for two years and reapply then. If I work hard, they might let me move to another field."

"Yes, of course," her mother said, trying to hide the shakiness in her voice. "Let's finish supper. We'll discuss this later."

Dana allowed herself to be pushed into the dining room, her heart sinking.

CHAPTER  TWO

By now, dear reader, you are probably wondering about the world in which Dana lives.

Some say it all began the day the people elected their president for the last time. Caught up in the historicalness of the moment, they used it as proof that the country had progressed forward. Anyone who questioned the qualifications of the man to be president was immediately scorned. Not wanting to be singled out, people voted for him, or remained silent.

But no one looked into his character. What did the man himself believe? Did he believe what he said, or did he just say what he knew people wanted to hear so as to win the election? No one knew anything about the man or his past, nor did they care. All they saw was an opportunity to elect a man people said would bring the world together. A man who was hip, with it, who understood them and their pain. A man who cared.

And so they did.

Parties reigned throughout the nation as people celebrated. Four years later, they reelected him. He had promised to make the wealthy pay for earning their money on the backs of the poor. He promised that no one would want for anything. Health care would be free, and everyone would have a job and own a home. There would be no poverty or suffering. People would live in paradise.

It was years later that the people realized who their "messiah" was. Taxes rose. Regulations increased to ensure that everything was fair and that everyone had a "fair shot". Businesses found themselves unable to meet the costs of doing business under this new leadership, so they closed. Unemployment rose as a result.

But the president was not discouraged. He said that the problem was the system. That if he had the authority, he could fix everything. So Congress relinquished its authority and so did the courts. Soon, all future elections were disbanded as unnecessary and too divisive, even though the president himself fueled the division. Despite his new authority and edicts, the president could not fix the problem. Not that he cared.

People soon found themselves in a world they did not understand. They had traded their freedom for security and received nothing. Riots broke out as the economy crumbled. Those who had nothing felt that they deserved the wealth of the rich. They staged protests, marching on the property of the wealthy. Eventually, the government came in and confiscated all wealth, saying that it belonged to the people and should be evenly distributed.

Despite all attempts, the economy suffered even more. As money became worthless and many were forced into poverty, riots broke out again across the nation. In an effort to contain it, the president dispatched the military. Once the gunfire ceased, all that remained were bodies.

Time passed, and like all men, the president eventually died. Soon after, disease broke out, decimating the population. Desperate, people turned to the government for help and answers.

In an effort to salvage what it could, the government did away entirely with the old system and set up a new one. A president was selected who would govern with a council. Bureaucratic bodies were set up to administer the slew of regulations that came forth. As the population dwindled from the epidemic, centers of progress were set up on the two coasts.

Desperate for relief, people flocked to them. As the interior of the country became vacated, the government decided it was not needed at all. A series of dust storms raged across that region, reinforcing their decision. It had become a barren wasteland due to a severe drought. They decided only the east and west coasts mattered because that was where people lived. A rail system was built to connect the two coasts and trains carried goods and supplies.

No one ventured to the interior of the country. It had become the territory of bandits and thieves. People who cared nothing for law and order. No man's land.

More time passed and people became comfortable with their new world order. Everything was regulated, but as long as they had a roof over their heads and food in their stomachs; they didn't care. The two coasts became the only civilized parts of the country. Everything was controlled. Everything was structured. People did as they were told. According to the government, this brought equality. This brought freedom, freedom from liberty.

CHAPTER THREE

When the street lights had gone out, Dana threw off the covers and slipped on her shoes. She opened the door to her room a crack, making certain that her parents were asleep. Her father's snore told her they were. Quickly, Dana opened her window and removed the screen. She crawled outside, hiding behind the bush that was there.

Glancing down the street, Dana dashed to the other side and down an alleyway. She kept to the shadows to avoid detection. Officers patrolled the streets at night. Anyone caught out past curfew was subject to prosecution. Mostly, they just disappeared and were never heard from again.

Dana did not care about the consequences. She wanted a place to think and knew just where to go.

She found the wall that marked the city limits. The area beyond was out of bounds, and none were supposed to venture there. Dana ran her hand against the concrete wall, looking for the place where a part of it had crumbled away. *Found it.* Carefully, she removed the loose bricks, revealing a hole just big enough to crawl through.

Once through, Dana waited for the guard tower spotlight to turn away. She ran off into the night, far away from her city and to the great beyond. Once she knew she was safely away, Dana slowed to a walk until she found the trail that her grandfather had once shown her. Following it, Dana knew where it would take her.

At last, she reached a small clearing that overlooked a valley and the city she lived in. Her home seemed so peaceful from where she stood. Dana sat on the soft grass and picked at the flowers.

"I don't want to go," she said to the night sky.

"Then don't," her grandfather's voice said in her mind.

Oftentimes, Dana imagined that he still answered her, even though he was dead. Years ago, when she was a small child, they came to the same clearing. He would take her and Lina in the middle of the night, and together, they snuck outside the city. Dana fiddled with her hair as she remembered how he would put it into two braids, calling her his "Indian Princess". Then, he would give her some strawberries that he had somehow managed to procure. She had loved those moments when they just sat together alone without the fear of being caught.

Sadness overtook her as she remembered the day her grandfather had left. He had fallen and broken his hip. The Board of Health had decided that it wasn't worth the cost of fixing it. He had become too old, a waste of resources. Soon afterward, he received a notice informing him to report to Wing 16 of the hospital. Everyone dreaded such a letter. All who went to Wing 16 never returned.

The day her family took her grandfather there was seared into her mind. Her mother wept quietly, trying to hide her tears. Though somber, her father managed to hold back his emotions as he held onto Lina. Dana did not understand at the time. She only knew that she would never see her beloved grandfather again.

"Don't cry for me," her grandfather had told her as he hugged her. "You must be brave, my little Indian Princess."

"I don't know how," Dana had cried.

"You have a greatness about you. You will change things." He kissed her and disappeared behind the steel doors of Wing 16.

Dana wiped a tear from her eye as she thought back to that time. Briefly, she considered running away. *But where will I go?* She shook her head. Dana knew she could not flee; her parents would suffer if she did.

The clock tower in the city tolled, telling her that she had lingered too long. Hastily, Dana left. She made her way back to the hole in the wall and slipped through. After replacing the bricks, she looked about for officers. Finding it clear, Dana went back home, slipped through her window, and went to bed. Tomorrow, her new life began.

Morning dawned and Dana found herself waiting at the bus depot with her parents. A somber mood overwhelmed them. They waited patiently for the bus to arrive that would take her to Waste Management.

Car ownership was illegal; it was considered bad for the environment, and the plant lay too far away for her to walk. Dana thought it odd that those within the government were allowed to own vehicles.

A horn sounded as the bus pulled up. Black smog erupted from the back end of the dingy bus. You'd think they could make a bus that didn't produce so much smoke, thought Dana.

Her mother's light touch forced her to turn around.

"It's alright, mom," said Dana in an effort to comfort her mother. "In two years, I'll apply for reassignment. I might even get it."

Her mother forced a weak smile. "Here," she wrapped a jacket around Dana's shoulders. "They always leave the windows open on that bus and it gets drafty. And take this." Her mother placed the strap of a bag on Dana's shoulders. "A little something for the road." Dana hugged her.

"You take care of yourself," her father said as he hugged her.

"I will, dad. Take care of yourselves too."

A tear welled up in his eyes. "My darling girl."

The sharp, impatient honk of the horn forced them to part. Dana climbed onto the bus and sat in a window seat toward the back. She waved one last time as the bus pulled away.

Dana peeked into the bag that her mother had given her. She found a thermos of milk and a small bag of cookies. Cookies were contraband items. Dana's heart ached as she realized that her mother risked everything to give her their weekly ration of milk and a forbidden treat.

The bus plowed through the city as it headed for the Waste Management plant, making stops along the way to pick up more unlucky graduates. Dana stared out the window as she munched her cookies. No one bothered to look in her direction.

They passed the Ministry Building, where a long line of new employees awaited initiation. Dana spotted Kenny. He wore a crisp suit that cost more than what most earned in a month. Jealousy filled her. At that moment, she found herself hating Kenny and his family, just because his father was the First Councilman and an influential man on the Careers Board because of his position, the very board that dealt out career assignments. As Dana thought about it, she realized that the kids whose parents ran the various bureaucratic agencies always got the most desirable positions.

She settled back into her uncomfortable seat as the bus continued. By midafternoon, they pulled into the Potomac Sector where the Waste Management plant was. Dana studied the old ruins of white buildings. Remnants of the old ways, a time when people failed to realize the equality of fairness.

Smoke filled the area, making it difficult to breathe. Dana covered her mouth with the sleeve of her jacket. Slowly, the bus pulled into the main part of the plant.

An officer stepped onto the bus the moment the doors opened. "Everyone off," she yelled. "Now! Move it!"

Instantly, people jumped from their seats and scrambled over each other to get off the bus. Dana found herself pushed and shoved into a line of others who were unlucky like her.

Another officer waited for them to line up. He paced before them in his crisp uniform and shiny black boots with a baton in his hands. "Listen up! My name is Officer Burroughs and I run this establishment. My word is law. Obey it and we will get along fine. Disobey, and suffer the consequences.

"Some of you may think you don't belong here. I don't give a damn what you think. You are here now and that is all that matters. This is where all the trash comes. We organize some for recycling, the rest is incinerated.

"You will all be divided into groups where you will sleep and live together in a barracks. You get two meals a day in the cafeteria. You will spend 14 hours a day working. One hour for relaxation. The rest is for sleeping.

"Those who receive permits to live together will be transferred to family housing."

Officer Burroughs pointed his baton in the direction of a bunch of shacks. Most of those buildings had one or two rooms and no electricity.

"There will be no leaving this place. The boundaries are clearly marked. Anyone who violates them will be dealt with accordingly.

"Welcome to Waste Management." He smiled sardonically.

Immediately, officers parceled everyone into groups. Dana soon found herself stripped of her belongings. She was glad she had eaten her mother's cookies on the bus. Soon, she was led naked through the plant, with others, to the showers. Men and women were shoved in the same showers in groups. They had 10 minutes to wash. Once finished, they were forced through a lice inspection before being given their work clothes, which consisted of a gray shirt, coveralls, and heavy boots.

Dana looked at a group of pregnant women who picked through the recycling pile as she marched to her barracks. After a quick tour of the plant, each received their work schedule.

"Deviation from the schedules is not allowed," said the officer that handed them out.

Dana studied hers, noting that she had to be at the incinerator at six in the morning. She plopped it and her blanket and pillow on a bunk.

"That's my bunk," said a voice behind her.

Dana turned and found a black kid of about her age, holding a blanket and pillow. She grabbed her stuff and moved to a different bunk, not wanting a fight.

"Hey, baby," said the kid, "I'm sure we can work something out." His eyes roamed up and down her slender form.

"I don't think so."

"Hey, no one turns their back on me. Now, baby, you may be brown skinned, but I could make an exception for you. See my boys back there. We could protect you if you were to be my girl."

"I'll pass," said Dana.

"Hey," the kid grabbed her wrist tightly, pulling her toward him.

Infuriated at being treated in such a way, she grabbed the back of his head and forced it into the bed post.

"You bitch!" The boy held his bloody nose. "I'll…"

"Is there a problem here?" A couple of officers had arrived, each waving their electric batons.

"Naw, man," said the kid, still holding his nose.

"Take your bunks," said the officer.

Dana snatched her stuff and moved to a bunk on the other end of the room.

"Hey, you bunk with us," said a dark-skinned girl with braids. A scrawny guy with glasses sat next to her.

Dana put her stuff on a nearby bunk.

"I'm Elsie," said the girl. "And this is Sanders. A total brainiac by the way."

"Dana."

"So, making enemies with Mad Dog over there? Way to go, genius."

"Mad Dog?" asked Dana.

"No one knows his real name. He's from the South like Sanders and I here. Same neighborhood actually."

"I can see why he was sent here."

"Hey, troublemakers are always sent here," said Elsie. "I got one too many citations and Sanders here, that's a laugh."

"Did you know that you can take a chip and use it to power a light bulb? In fact…"

"She gets the point, Sanders," said Elsie.

"If you're really good with technology, shouldn't you have been assigned to the Science and Technological Research Division?" Dana asked.

"He was," said Elsie, "but they kicked him out."

"Why?"

"I told them they still practiced the primitive stone age of computers. His figures were based on outdated logarithms of…"

"The point is," interrupted Elsie, "he questioned the authorities, so they sent him here. What about you?"

"I ask too many questions," said Dana.

"Whoa! That'll do it."

"Lights out!" yelled an officer as everything went dark.

"Will you take the top bunk?" said Sanders. "I'm afraid of heights."

"It's as tall as your head," said Elsie. "Oh, very well." She climbed into the top bunk while Dana nestled into hers. "See ya in the morning."

CHAPTER FOUR

Morning came all too early for Dana. She felt like she had just fallen asleep when the officers burst in, banging their batons on the sides of the bed.

"Everyone up! Now!"

One by one, people sat up, rubbing the sleep from their eyes. Mad Dog glared at Dana as she put on her clothes. Since privacy was nonexistent in the barracks, Dana didn't care if he saw her naked. He probably already had after the mandatory group showers.

The grungy coveralls smelled of filth. Dana wondered if they were ever washed, or if someone had recently worn these before she was issued them.

"To the mess hall!"

Dana looked at one of the officers. *They really run a tight schedule.* She quickly grabbed her boots and started to the eating hall with Elsie and Sanders.

Mad Dog bumped right into her, pushing her into the wall. "Excuse me," he spat.

Dana scowled at him as she rubbed her newly formed bruise. She knew he did it on purpose.

"Just ignore him," said Elsie, pulling her along.

Breakfast consisted of brown slop. Dana wrinkled her nose at it. It smelled awful, but she took it. One scoop per bowl. No seconds allowed.

Together, the three new friends sat down at one of the long tables. Dana played with her food a bit. "What is this?"

"You're better off not knowing," said the man sitting next to her. "Believe me, in time, you will look forward to eating this stuff."

"It smells horrible," said Sanders.

"Just chew and swallow," said the man. "Don't think about it."

"Thanks," said Dana.

"Name's George Saule." The man held out his hand. He had graying hair and looked to be in his 50s, though Dana really couldn't tell. She figured a place like this would prematurely age anyone.

"Dana," said Dana. "How long have you been here?"

"Forty years," replied George, "give or take a few."

"No talking," roared an officer. "You have 10 minutes to eat before your shift."

Dana looked around at the uniformed officers that patrolled the area. She was used to officers being everywhere. Even at home, one never escaped them, but this was different. There were more of them, and they cracked down on anything that smacked of breaking the rules. She surveyed the armed guards that stood at various points of the eating hall. These men wore helmets and body armor, probably so you can't see their faces, thought Dana. The thought that they were more prisoners than workers prickled Dana's mind.

"Don't mind them," said George. Some of the slop dripped from his whiskers as he shoveled more into his mouth. "They just don't like people getting to know one another. If you get to know someone, you might start to like them. To think of them as human."

"But we are human," said Elsie.

"Not to them," said George. "The moment you got shipped here, you ceased to be human. Now you're just animals to them. Workhorses."

Dana didn't like that thought at all. She quickly ate what was in her bowl. Her stomach growled after she had finished; she was clearly still hungry. *Why is it we are never allowed our fill?* Before an officer could bang their baton on the table, she quickly took her bowl to the dish drop-off. A scrawny man took it. His vacant eyes said it all. He had been here treated as nothing more than a piece of meat for too long.

Dana stared at him and his hollow eyes. Methodically, he took her bowl and put it in the sink. His demeanor haunted her the rest of the day. She studied those around her. They possessed the same hollow expression. Only the newbies had any ounce of life, something she was sure would soon be beaten out of them.

"Get to work!"

Dana darted off after being yelled at again by another officer. She reported to the duty station where she received her tools for the day's work.

That day, she was to work with the incinerator. Dana

didn't like it. The noise pounded her ears, giving her a head-ache. She didn't know where Elsie and Sanders had gone. Dana guessed that they were scheduled to work elsewhere.

"So we meet again," said George as she reported for duty.

"Um, yeah," said Dana.

"Don't worry," said George, "I'll help you through, seeing as how this is your first day and all."

Dana put on her workman's gloves and held onto her rake.

"See this?" George pointed at a chute above them. "This is where the garbage comes out of from the level above. The people up there sort through what's brought in. What's to be recycled goes elsewhere. The rest comes to us. When you hear the alarm, make sure you are clear; otherwise, you'll get crushed."

"What comes out of there, we put into the incinerator."

George pointed at the hole in the ground with large fires in it. Dana leaned over some to look.

"Don't lean too far," warned George. "If you fall in there, you're dead."

A screeching sound filled the area.

"Clear out of the way," said George, pulling Dana back.

Instantly, a hole above them opened and out poured all sorts of garbage. The smell gagged Dana as she tried to not breathe it in. George acted as though it didn't bother him. Clinking bottles and metal hit the ground around them as mounds of refuse formed a gigantic pile. Once the alarms ceased and the chute above them closed, people moved in with their rakes and began pushing it into the incinerator.

"Well, time to work," said George as he raked piles of junk into the fires below them.

Dana started raking in some papers. At first, she took

her time, afraid of falling into the incinerator. After a while, the officers on duty grew tired of her wariness. In an attempt to catch up, Dana just shoved stuff into the fires, not caring what made it in there. Just don't let me slip and fall, she thought to herself.

The heat from the fires made her throat ache for water, but she could not satisfy it. They only had one water boy on their floor and he could barely keep up with the demands for it.

Pausing momentarily, Dana wiped the sticky sweat from her face. Her clothes clung to her skin, forming damp folds around her body. The dampness did little to cool her down. After about an hour, the heat began to make her lightheaded. Noticing this, George told her to sit for a while.

"Here," he said, giving her a canteen of water. "You drink that, but don't let the officers catch you. Strictly speaking, I'm not supposed to have that."

Dana took a big swig, grateful to have something liquid to put down her throat. It had a lemon taste to it, and she wondered where he got it. She looked over and saw a set of huge gears grinding away. "What are those?" Dana asked.

George looked at where she pointed. "Those are the grinders," he said. "Stay away from them if you can. Get too close and you might get sucked in. Many a man was killed or worse from those things."

"I thought we had safety laws," said Dana, foolishly.

George laughed. "Who told you that? Your teachers? The only safety laws are for the bureaucrats. People who work in this place, or the other manual labor jobs, are lucky if they see tomorrow. One thing you should always keep in mind: those who put you here are hoping you will die here."

An officer appeared from around a corner. Quickly, George snatched his canteen and hauled Dana to her feet. He immediately started shoveling refuse into the fires. Dana copied his movements while keeping a wary eye on the officer.

She noticed something hanging from George's neck. Never knowing a man to wear jewelry, Dana allowed her curiosity to get the better of her. "What's that you're wearing?"

George looked where she pointed. "Nothing." He shoved it under his shirt. Dana let it drop.

A spot of red caught her attention. A girl of about seven with flaming red hair hid behind some metal barrels. Her wide, blue eyes bore into Dana, pleading for something.

Suddenly, Dana was reminded of her older sister. Separated by a year, they had been very close. Her sister, Lina, had red hair just like the young girl that studied her. Six years ago, Lina was diagnosed with cancer.

Dana remembered the day she came home from school and was told the news. The first round of chemotherapy went well, but then the cancer worsened. Despite many appeals to the health board, it was determined that to try and cure Lina would be a waste of resources. The day they got the summons for Wing 16 of the hospital was the day her mother cried the most.

Dana thought her heart had been ripped apart the day they said good-bye to her grandfather. It was irreparably broken after they had to deliver Lina.

"Don't cry," Lina had told her. "You need to be strong now. Like grandfather said, we'll see each other again."

Refusing to lose Lina, Dana's father decided to smuggle her out of the city. Others had tried to avoid the summons to Wing 16, but officers just came and got them. The same happened to Lina. That night, alone in her room, Dana cried until her pillow dripped from the tears.

"Hey!" George pulled her from her memories. "Stay in the present, or you'll get killed."

"George, who is that?"

George glanced at the red-haired girl watching them. "She's Jesse, a waste-rat."

"A what?"

"Waste-rat. That's what they call children who are born here. There are some shacks just outside this facility where people who want to marry are allowed to live. They're mostly one-room establishments. Anyway, any children that are born to them are called waste-rats. They're born here and they die here. This is all they ever know. Many of them become orphans by the time they're seven."

"Why would anyone want to bring children into this place?" asked Dana without thinking.

"Why does anyone try to have a family?" replied George. "There is this human need to want a family. It's built into each of us. I guess some here choose to do it because they hope for the future. They hope that the future will be better than the present."

"Did you consider having a family?" The moment Dana asked that, she knew she shouldn't have. George's face contorted into a mixture of rage and sorrow. "Sorry, it's none of my business."

Dana grabbed her rake and continued shoving piles of garbage into the roaring fires that reached out for it.

A commotion arose across the way. Dana saw one of the grates under other workers shift. It hovered precariously over the fires. It lurched again.

"Get out! Get out!"

Shouts and yells went up all around as the floor beneath Dana's feet quaked and thunder rumbled beneath her feet.

"It's gonna blow!"

Workers fled, dropping their rakes and running as fast as possible. Unsure of what was happening, Dana just stood there watching everything. The floor beneath her lurched again and tipped toward the fires.

Dana's feet slipped on the refuse she stood on, and instantly, she started falling toward the flames. Desperately, she reached out for anything as she slid closer to certain death.

A strong hand seized hers. Dana latched onto it as George pulled her to safety. "We need to get out of here!"

George shoved Dana away from the incinerator as an ominous gurgling noise filled the area below. Her feet slipped and slid on the piles of greasy garbage they were forced to run on. Others darted past her, having more experience in this matter.

A terrified scream reached Dana's ears. She looked over and saw a man hanging precariously from a rail. If he lost his grip, he would fall into the incinerator.

Glancing around, Dana watched as people stood frozen despite the man's pleas for help. Without thinking, she rushed for him.

"Dana! No!" yelled George.

She didn't listen. It just didn't seem right letting that man die because she was too scared to help. Her feet sank deep within the piles of garbage as she ran for the man crying for help.

Officers just watched the proceedings with mild interest. They had already gotten to safety and had no desire to help any of the workers.

"Help me, please!"

Dana skidded to her knees as she reached the man hanging above the flames. She took hold of his arms. "Don't worry. I'm here."

A flame burst from the fire below, stretching up and reaching the ceiling. The heat of it burned Dana's skin, but she ignored it.

"Take my hand."

The man grasped her sweaty palm as Dana seized him with her other hand. She heaved on the man, but he weighed too much. She slid closer to the flames. Her muscles strained against gravity as they moved closer to the incinerator beneath them.

The fear in the man's eyes etched itself onto Dana's memory. He knew he was going to die, and she too. Once again, she pulled him up. Slowly, they started to pull away from the hole that led to the incinerator.

Without warning, a huge explosion rocked the area. The force of it knocked Dana back, sending her flying through the air until she crashed into the hard wall. Agonizing screams from the man she had tried to save echoed in her ears as he was burned alive and fell into the flames below. Dazed, Dana watched as her efforts to save a life quickly burned to ash.

An officer walked up to her. "We were wondering if you would succeed," he said. "We even took bets. I won."

Dana stared after him in disbelief as he walked away counting his money.

George came up to her and hauled her to her feet. He did a quick check to make certain she wasn't permanently injured. "That was foolish," he scolded. "You need to learn that life is cheap here."

Wiping a trickle of blood from her forehead, Dana

refused to hold back her anger. "If I ran like the rest of you, I would be no better than those officers."

When the shift ended, the buzzer sounded, signaling quitting time. Dana followed the others and put away her rake and gloves. Her stomach ached from hunger. She had had only one meal that day and had worked at least 12 hours.

Thoughts of the man dying in front of her filled her mind, and instantly, her hunger died away. "Why?" she thought. It all seemed so pointless.

She fiddled with her bowl of brown sludge. If this was life in Waste Management, then Dana wanted none of it. A mop of red hair caught her attention. Jesse had snuck into the eating hall and watched hungrily as everyone ate. Dana took the slice of bread they had been given and wrapped it in a napkin. She wasn't very hungry.

Making certain that none of the officers watched her, Dana took her supper and walked over to the girl who hid behind a giant trash can in the shadows. "Here," she said, kneeling down and holding out her food. "Go on. Take it."

Jesse's nimble fingers grasped the bowl and the bread with a strength that Dana didn't think she possessed. She ran away and disappeared around a corner. Dana stood up and headed back to the barracks.

Elsie and Sanders waited for her. "Hey," she said, "we heard about today and the explosion."

They had been assigned to the recycling section of the plant and had not witnessed the explosion of the incinerator.

"Yeah," said Dana.

"Well, tell us," Elsie insisted.

"A man was killed," said Dana somberly. "The incinerator blew up and everyone panicked. One man fell in. I tried to save him, but..."

"Oh, Dana, I'm so sorry," Elsie put her hand over her mouth in shock. "I knew you had been scheduled to work there, but I never thought..."

"The thing is, no one else bothered to help him," continued Dana. "Even as he hung there, people just worried about themselves. But that wasn't the most sickening thing."

"What was?" asked Sanders.

"The officers had taken bets as to whether I would be able to save him or not," replied Dana. "One even thanked me for allowing him to win."

"That is sick," grunted Elsie. "This whole place is disgusting."

"But this is life," said Sanders. "How are we to change it when everyone accepts it? The ones in charge aren't about to change."

"Well, maybe there is nothing we can do, but I wish there was." Elsie's eyes brightened a bit as she remembered something. "Hey, I noticed you didn't eat anything. Here." She handed Dana a slice of bread that she had snitched from the kitchens.

"Where did you get this?" asked Dana.

"Don't worry about it," said Elsie. "Eat it. Quick, before anyone sees you."

Dana thanked her friend and chowed down on the bread. Despite its stale flavor and crustiness, her mouth appreciated it as her stomach had reawakened to its hunger.

"Lights out!"

Dana shoved the remaining bread crust in her mouth before the officer noticed her. She slipped under the blanket on her bunk and fell fast asleep, exhausted from the day's events.

CHAPTER FIVE

A soft hand covered Dana's mouth. She jerked awake, but the small, delicate hand held her still. Dana looked over and Jesse stood over her with her finger over her mouth. Realizing that something was terribly wrong, Dana sat up. Jesse motioned for her to follow.

Making certain that no one watched, Dana slipped on her shoes. She headed for the exit, but Jesse caught her arm. She pointed at a hole in the wall and slipped through. Hurriedly, Dana followed.

They darted across the open field in the darkness to the barbed wire fence. The guards were too preoccupied with a poker game. Jesse pointed at a loose wire in the fence. She bent it and wriggled through. With a little extra effort, Dana did the same. Quickly, Jesse repositioned the wire so that it looked as strong as the others.

She ran off into the night towards what was called Shackville. Dana followed wondering why the girl had woken her. They reached the mass of trailers and small huts within minutes. Fires filled trash cans as people huddled around them with forlorn faces. One mother hugged her baby as she attempted to keep warm on the chilly night.

Skin and bones, thought Dana. She didn't see any officers patrolling the area. She figured that the authorities didn't worry about these people. They were probably too tired and too starved to attempt to flee anywhere.

They ran past shanty buildings that people called home. Jesse knew where she was going and all Dana could do was follow. After a few twists and turns, they came upon a small shack that was a mix of metal pieces and boards put together with nails.

Jesse opened the door and let Dana in.

"Nana is sick," said Jesse.

Dana looked over at the cot in the place. An elderly woman lay on it coughing. Not knowing what to do, Dana felt the woman's forehead. It burned. Dana figured that her kindness earlier made Jesse think she could help.

"I need water," said Dana.

Jesse left the room and came back minutes later with a bucket of water.

Dana looked at the black mess. She snatched another container and wiped it out as best she could. Then, she took her shirt and placed it over the empty container. Carefully, she poured the water from the full bucket into the empty one, using her shirt as a filter.

"Boil this," said Dana as she handed the newly filtered water to Jesse.

Dana shook her shirt and put it back on. Jesse walked back in. "Is it boiling?"

"It will in about 10 minutes."

"I need a plant. It looks like this." Dana drew a picture in the dirt on the floor. "Do you have anything like that here?"

Jesse nodded and ran out.

Frowning, Dana looked at the woman on the cot. She hoped her efforts helped. Dana remembered a time when her mother was called to help a neighbor with a fever. She had done the same as what Dana attempted now.

Jesse ran back in with several weeds in her hand that resembled what Dana had tried to draw.

"Put those in the boiling water," said Dana. "When it has steeped for five minutes, and the water looks green, bring it to me."

Dana brought the only oil lamp in the room closer. *No electricity*. Sorrow filled her at the idea of how these people were forced to live. And she thought she had it bad growing up. At least her family was allowed electricity, even if it was regulated.

The old woman shivered despite the on her brow. Gently, Dana dabbed the woman's forehead.

Jesse walked back in with the cast iron pot full of newly made tea.

Dana took it from the girl, who barely managed to carry it. She found a somewhat clean spoon. Carefully, she lifted the water to the woman's mouth and poured some in. Liquid drizzled down the woman's cheek as it seeped from her lips.

Satisfied that she got enough of it down the old woman, Dana put the pot down and waited. There was little else for her to do. Now it was up to the old woman and nature.

She nestled on the floor in a corner, not wanting to leave the woman alone. Jesse curled in her lap whimpering.

"Shh, don't cry," soothed Dana wiping the girl's tears. "It will be alright."

"But Nana has been sick a long time."

Dana rocked the small girl and sang to her. She sang the same lullaby that her grandfather had sung to her mother, that her mother had sung to her and her sister.

> Sweet child, dry your tears.
> Cast away all your fears.
> Listen to the gentle wind
> As its song will never end.
> Sleep now, under the willow.
> Sleep now, safe in nature's cello.

Hours later, a grunting noise woke Dana. She looked up and saw the old woman staring at her.

"I told her not to, but she never listens," said the woman.

"I'm sorry..."

"Just call me Nana. Everyone else does."

Dana carefully stood up, taking care not to wake the sleeping Jesse as she laid the girl on the floor. "She came to me last night in the barracks and I couldn't refuse her."

"So you're the one that gave her the food," said Nana. "She brought it here for me to eat." Nana glanced at Jesse, who still slept soundly. "She is such a kind child. She doesn't deserve this life."

"Are you her mother?"

"I'm too old for children," sighed Nana. "No, I knew her

mother and father before they died. Her father was killed in an accident at the plant. Her mother died weeks later from a broken heart. No one wanted a waif. God, there are so many of them here, and most can barely feed themselves. But I took her in. And now I am afraid I must leave her too."

"What do you mean?" asked Dana.

"Child, I have been sick a long time." A series of deep, congested coughs filled the room. "I have tuberculosis. It has gotten worse these past several months and it's only a matter of time now."

"But there is medicine that could cure you," exclaimed Dana.

"Yes, but who is going to allocate precious resources to an old woman like me? I am a waste-rat, just like you are now. All who are sent here are sent here to die."

Dana thought back on the man that had burned to death before her eyes. The truth of Nana's statement sounded all too familiar.

"I thank you for your help," said Nana.

The sun peeked over the horizon, and horror filled Dana as she realized that she would be late for duty. She did not want to find out what punishment would be in store for her at such an offense. "I need to get back before they know I'm gone."

"Jesse will help you."

The girl woke up and smiled at seeing her Nana feeling better.

"She needs to get back," said Nana to Jesse.

The girl jumped to her feet and motioned for Dana to follow. She didn't say much, but the intelligence in her eyes said it all.

As they ran through the dirty streets of Shackville, a man throwing waste water out his door caught Dana's eye.

It was George. She couldn't understand why he lived there, unless he always lived there.

They locked eyes for a moment and Dana stopped running. A pipe hung from George's mouth as he watched her. A small tug on her arm reminded her that she had to go.

Pulling herself away, Dana followed Jesse back to the hole in the fence. She squeezed through, but Jesse did not follow.

"Aren't you coming?" asked Dana.

Jesse shook her head. "Stick to the shadows and no one will see you." The red-haired girl ran off.

Knowing she did not have time to waste, Dana sprinted away, doing as Jesse had ordered. She hunkered low to the ground, sticking to the sides of buildings and the shadows they offered. The sun had not fully risen yet, which helped.

Soon Dana came upon the hole in the wall to her barracks. She squeezed through and placed a crate in front of it to conceal it. The snoring in the room told her that the buzzer had not sounded. Tiptoeing, she crept to her bunk and sat upon it just as the officers burst into the room.

"Everyone up!"

The fluorescent lights flickered on. Groggily, people sat up, rubbing the sand from their eyes. Elsie studied Dana's muddied shirt and shoes. "Where have you been?"

"Nowhere," replied Dana as she changed into her coveralls.

The expression on Elsie's face indicated her disbelief, but she let the matter drop.

Dana went to her locker in the shower room. She opened hers up and found her soap missing.

"Looking for this?" said Mad Dog, holding up the bar of soap. He and his friends laughed and jeered at her.

"Give it back," said Dana.

"Think I'll keep it as recompense for breaking my nose," replied Mad Dog. "Besides, no amount of bathing will rid your odor."

Dana slammed her locker shut. Angered, she toyed with the idea of charging him.

Elsie arrived on the scene before Dana could make a choice. "Give it back, Mad Dog."

"What are you, Elsie? Her bodyguard?"

"I said to give it back," Elsie held out her hand. Something in her demeanor commanded respect. Even Mad Dog seemed frightened.

Backing down, he handed her the soap. "Fine. Take it."

Elsie gave Dana the soap, who quickly put it in her locker.

"Why'd he back down like that?" asked Dana.

"Because of my father," said Elsie. "One day, Mad Dog and his friends jumped me. My father beat the crap out of all of them. Ever since then, they've left me alone. Come on, let's get some breakfast."

That day, Dana was scheduled to work in the recycling center of the plant. She rifled through the junk she stood upon, separating the metal from paper and plastic from glass. The rest went into the chute for those in the incineration section.

She strained as she lifted up a particularly heavy piece of metal.

"Here," said Sanders, as he grabbed the other end.

Together, they tossed it aside into the scrap metal pile. It would be melted down in another section of the plant.

"Elsie says that you weren't in your bed all night," said Sanders.

Dana frowned. "I was hoping she hadn't noticed."

"Where were you?"

An officer strolled past and they quickly bent down, each picking up some piece of trash. Once the officer had disappeared, they resumed talking.

"I met this little girl, Jesse. Her grandmother has gotten very ill and she came to find me. I couldn't refuse."

"Did you cure her?" asked Sanders, truly concerned about Nana.

"No," said Dana. "She needs medicine. The kind that we are never given unless we're important enough."

"What does she have?"

"Tuberculosis."

"I know exactly what she needs," said Sanders. "But there is only one place to get it and I haven't located it."

"Where?"

"The underground market," replied Sanders, as though it should have been obvious.

Of course, thought Dana, the black market. Where else would she get something she needed? The trouble was, you had to know someone who knew where it was. They kept their location secret.

Dana noticed George moving a cart full of plastic scraps. She noticed the canteen of his sticking out of his pocket. It hit her. He knew where the underground market was. Where else did he get the stuff he put in his canteen? It wasn't issued.

Abandoning her station, Dana darted across the space to George. Her boots pounded the ground beneath her, slipping and sliding on bits of cardboard. Making sure no officers saw her, Dana grabbed George and pinned him against the wall.

"What the…"

"Where is the underground market?" demanded Dana.

"What?"

"I know you know where it is. Don't deny it."

Surprised by her strength and resolve, George relented. "Why would I tell you?"

"I have a friend who is ill. She needs medicine and that is the only place to get it."

"And how are you going to pay for it?"

Dana's grip loosened. She hadn't thought of that. Payment. Everything came with a price.

"I can take you to it, but unless you have a form of payment, it won't do you much good."

"How much?" asked Dana.

"Something like medicine will cost a lot," replied George. "Now let me go."

Dana released him. "What if I'm able to find the money?"

"Then come find me and we'll talk then."

George gripped his cart and pushed it away, leaving Dana alone without a clue as to where she would find the money she needed.

CHAPTER

SIX

Elsie and Dana clung to the dump truck as it moved throughout the city, making frequent stops for them to grab the canisters of garbage. They pulled up into a posh, luxurious multistory building.

"You girls will have to go in there and collect the bins. Pour their contents in the chute and then leave. There is a bin on each floor. And hurry up!" The driver settled back in his truck.

"And don't dawdle. These people don't like our kind in their building."

Elsie and Dana went inside. They walked up to the front desk of the lobby. The guy at the desk gave them a disgusted expression. He scanned their chips and allowed them to pass.

"You are to empty the bins on each floor," said the man at the front desk. "The faster you get it done, the better. Folk around here don't like seeing you people."

You people, thought Dana. In school, she was taught that the collective group was a family; each member had their proper role and all were to be respected, though she and others knew that the equality in their society was more words than reality.

"And don't touch anything," mocked Elsie as they climbed the stairs to the upper floors. "Folk around here don't like seeing you people around. Yeah, but they love having us empty their trash and clean up after them."

"Keep it down," said Dana.

"Why?"

"If anyone hears you, then we will both get in trouble."

Elsie paused on the stairwell. A pensive look crossed her face as she thought for several moments, making Dana nervous. "There's something wrong about that?"

"What?"

"Well, think about it," said Elsie, "We got sent to Waste Management because we asked too many questions, or refused to follow the rules. We cannot speak our minds without the fear of someone overhearing us and reporting us to an officer."

Elsie's words rang true and Dana knew it. She had spent her whole life afraid of speaking her mind for fear of punishment. When she did voice her opinion, she always got lectured. But school was a thing of the past, and now she was considered an adult. Punishment here was more than a lecture.

Dana thought back to Career Assignment Day and the man next door who was arrested as his wife cried in the street. His crime? He wrote a petition demanding the right to choose his own line of work and to be allowed to keep all of what he earned.

"You're right, Elsie," said Dana.

"Of course I'm right."

"But keep it down, for now. We have a job to do, and if we take too long, you know what will happen."

"All right," relented Elsie. "Here's the first floor."

"Actually," said Dana, stopping her, "why don't we go all the way to the top and work our way down? That way, we'll be on the bottom floor by the time we're worn out."

"Now that is first-rate thinking," said Elsie.

They hiked up the stairs in the coldly lit stairwell. Only non-essential personnel used the stairs. Those who actually worked at the building in the offices were allowed to use the elevator. Their feet slapped the linoleum of the floor as they ran to the top floor.

Exhausted, they stopped on the top step as they caught their breath. They panted heavily, taking long, slow, and deep breaths to slow their pulse.

"I hate stairs," gasped Elsie.

Dana agreed.

They opened the door to the top floor and met a sight completely different from anything they had ever seen. The entire area had whimsical decorations. Paintings lined the wall. Desks split into groups of four, and each had a comfortable chair. Computers and the latest gadgets covered every surface.

Dana couldn't believe it. In Waste Management, she was lucky to have a clean set of clothes and a hot meal. But here, these people wore very expensive clothes and wasted their time on electronic toys that she could never dream of owning.

Those working on the floor paused to glance at them. Their looks said it all. Elsie and Dana were not welcome.

"The bins are over there," said one woman, pointing to the other side of the room. "And don't forget the one in the banquet hall this time."

Both Elsie and Dana walked across the fancy rugs that covered the floor, their muddied boots leaving prints. They stood out with their grimy coveralls amidst the aristocratic and clean environment.

It took the efforts of both Dana and Elsie to empty the garbage bin down the chute. It thudded on the floor as they dropped it and rolled it back into place. A few faces turned toward them, giving them unpleasant looks.

"Here," said a man, handing Dana a half empty bottle of juice. "Take care of this for me."

Dana just stood there holding the bottle. *Is he incapable of throwing it away himself?*

"Pocket it," whispered Elsie.

Dana did so. The bottle fit easily in the deep pockets of her overalls.

Together, she and Elsie went into the banquet hall. It was used for meetings, parties, or just any excuse to chat and not work. Dana walked through the door and stopped aghast at what she saw.

On the one long table in the room were platters full of sweets. A tiered centerpiece held candies, pastries, and bits of fruit and cheese cut up in decorative bite-size pieces. She found another plate full of brownies and a third with a triple layer chocolate cake. On another table in the room was a sandwich station. Meats of every variety, cheeses, bread, condiments, and lettuce sat in pristine containers. Another section of the room had three gold-plated containers filled with soup.

Dana's stomach grumbled. She had lost weight since being sent to Waste Management. Her hand reached out for a brownie just as a rotund man walked in. She jerked her arm back.

The man went over to the soup bar and filled a crystal bowl with the stuff. He had gotten some of the soup on his fingers and licked them as he grabbed a spoon and napkin. The man paused by the brownie dish. Quickly, he snatched one and walked out without saying a word.

"I don't get it," said Elsie. "These foods are forbidden under the law of health equality. If I got caught with one of these, I'd be arrested. Yet, these people have it here, and they can eat anytime they want."

Jealousy rose within Dana. All her life, what she ate and did had been controlled in the name of public safety and equality. But these people were allowed to ignore all that without the consequences.

"We should take some," said Elsie, reaching out for a pastry.

Dana caught her arm. "What if we get caught?"

Just then, a young man of about Dana's age walked in with a rag. He stopped short and studied them a moment before going over to the soup bar and cleaning the mess that the man had made.

Dana instantly realized who he was. The building had caretakers, janitors, and cooks, all of whom were to remain unseen, but keep the area clean and maintained. She studied the man. He looked just as underfed as her. By his body language, Dana could tell that he wanted to reach out for the treats, but refused to since they were there.

"We won't tell anyone," said Dana.

He looked at her.

"Look, we're just as hungry as you and are only here for the trash bin. We'll just empty it and leave and then you can do what you want."

She and Elsie reached for the big garbage can and emptied it down the chute. Once they had put it back in its corner, they started for the door. A hand grabbed Dana's arm. The man held out a napkin with two brownies and pastries wrapped in it. His eyes flickered to the door, making certain no one walked in on them.

Dana took the small bundle. "Thank you."

The man snitched a pastry and darted away through another door that was barely noticeable among the wallpaper.

Dana tugged on Elsie, indicating that they should go. The two of them hid their treats in their pockets and hurried to the stairwell. She stopped short when she ran into Kenny.

"Kenny!"

People looked in their direction. Kenny quickly snatched her hand and pulled her to a secluded area.

"Kenny," said Dana. "What are you doing here?"

"My job," he said.

Dana noted that he seemed to have put on a little weight since they last saw each other.

"My father is doing one of his inspections and I accompanied him. It's part of my job. What are you doing here?"

"My job," said Dana. "This is my day for collecting garbage in the city."

Kenny noticed the slight bulge in Dana's pocket. He reached for it and she stopped him.

"Did you take food?"

Dana eyed Kenny with a piercing look.

"You could get arrested for that," said Kenny.

"Which would be far better than my current situation," replied Dana. "Do you know what life is like in Waste Management? We barely get enough to eat, and we spend the entire day by the fires disposing of items that you all decided were worth little more that the dirt you stand on."

Kenny let his arm drop. "Is it that bad?"

Dana said nothing.

Elsie coughed in the distance, indicating that they had wasted enough time.

"I've got to go," said Dana. "If I take too long, I'll be punished."

"Here." Kenny held out his watch to her. Dana studied it. It was a very expensive watch, which would fetch a good price in the underground market.

"What's this?"

"Take it," said Kenny. "I know there is an underground and they only deal with useable goods. My father talks about them all the time. Take it. Use it to get yourself something to eat."

Dana took the watch, holding it as confusion filled her. "Why are you doing this?"

"You're different, Dana," replied Kenny. "Different from the others around here."

Another bout of coughing from Elsie pulled Dana from her desire to ask questions. "Thanks," she said as she darted off.

Once in the stairwell, Elsie and Dana stopped and pulled out their snacks. Without wasting any time, they ate them so quickly that they barely registered the taste.

Their hunger satisfied, they trooped down to the next level and emptied the bins there. For the next hour, they repeated the process until they finally entered the lobby again.

An irate truck driver awaited them as they exited the building. "What took so long?" he demanded.

"Sorry," said Elsie. "Some of the containers were fuller than usual and very heavy to lift."

"Well, I suggest you hurry up next time," said the driver. "Get on."

Dana and Elsie hopped on the back of the dump truck, clinging to the bar that was there as it bounced down the road to the next collection.

The buildings of the city whizzed by as the wind ripped through Dana's hair. They soon pulled into the hospital. There was always a lot of garbage at hospitals.

"In and out," said the driver.

Dana and Elsie ran inside. Once again, they were greeted by someone at the front desk who scanned their chips and waved them through. Dana and Elsie did the bottom floor first. They walked through the waiting room of sick patients all waiting for their chance to see a doctor. Most would be sent home that day empty-handed.

Coughing and groaning filled the area. Dana scanned the pale faces in the room. One man wheezed so hard that she didn't think he'd live long enough to see a doctor.

"Walk-ins," said Elsie, "or the ones not lucky enough to be approved for an appointment. So they come here and wait for a doctor who might have a free moment."

Dana listened to Elsie explain the situation as though she had no clue what went on. She remembered all too well the suffering of those forced to be walk-ins. When her sister became constantly ill, the Board of Medicine refused to grant them more appointments. Eventually, they received the summons to Wing 16.

They darted past Wing 16 to get to the garbage bins. Dana watched as a mother dropped her toddler son at the doors. The crying woman did her best to shield her tears, but was unable to.

"What's wrong, mommy?" asked the boy.

"Nothing, my dear," said the woman. "Nothing. You must go with these people."

Two orderlies grabbed the boy and shoved him through the metal doors, not giving the mother a chance to say good-bye. Only those summoned actually saw what went on in there. The woman leaned on the doors, weeping uncontrollably.

"Come on," said Elsie, snatching Dana's arm. "There's nothing you can do."

They continued, passing a giant room filled with hospital beds and sick patients. Doctors and nurses rushed around trying to tend to them, but there were more patients than doctors. Crammed in like sardines, Dana pitied them. An ailing old woman stared at her as she walked by.

"Mrs. Goodwin, you are being released from the hospital," said a physician.

"But I'm not well," pleaded the woman.

"I'm sorry," said the physician, "but your treatment has been denied. Discharge her, nurse."

Dana noted the frustration in the doctor's voice at being forced to send a patient home without the chance of being able to help her. She continued on. Soon, she and Elsie found the garbage cans. One by one, they emptied them down the chute, ignoring the stench and green slime with white fuzz.

"Let's hurry," said Elsie. "That driver was pretty mad when we took so long the last time."

They burst into the stairwell and raced up the stairs, taking two at a time. They stopped when they reached the upper level of the hospital. Neither of them had ever been in there. This was the level for those deemed useful to society. Basically, if a patient was an official, or could bribe enough officials, they were sent here.

Together, she and Dana walked through the hall. Each patient had a private room with an open window, allowing them to look outside. The doctors seemed relaxed, not over-worked liked the ones on the level below.

Dana paused, looking into one room. A man with cancer received his treatment and a three-course meal. His family sat around him talking and laughing. Jealously filled Dana as she watched the man's children laugh and play as though they had no worries.

She read the tag on the door. "John Henderson, Board of Health." No wonder, thought Dana, because he was a member of the Board of Health, he received the cure while others were allowed to die.

The room next door contained a heart patient. Dana remembered seeing his face on the news being interviewed by Halloway. He was the head of the Monetary Management Board.

"Come on," hissed Elsie, grabbing Dana's arm once again. "Do you want us to get in trouble?"

"My sister should have been allowed here," said Dana.

"You know why she wasn't," replied Elsie.

Dana knew, but she hated it.

They found the bins on that level, fuller than the ones below. Together, the two girls heaved the bins into the chute, emptying them. Relieved that the load had been lightened, they plopped it back in its spot.

"Okay, let's get out of here," said Elsie. "This place depresses me."

"Agreed," said Dana.

They ran back to the stairs and charged down them. Quickly, the two ran outside past all of the ailing patients and frustrated doctors. No one noticed their presence, or that they had left. Invisible to all, that was what Dana and Elsie were.

They jumped back on the back of the dump truck, their fingers wrapping around the freezing metal bar. Once again, the driver started up the engine. Bouncing and jerking down the road, Dana observed the people as they drove by them. The well-dressed ones held their heads high, knowing that they had nothing to worry about, so long as they didn't question too much.

Others wore dirtier clothes: the janitors, waiters, and servants of the world. Servants like her. She knew what they felt, what they thought. Dana thought the same. *Where was my choice?*

CHAPTER SEVEN

The clatter of pots and utensils bounced off the concrete walls as Dana stood in line with the others waiting for their supper. She held out the bowl on her tray. This time, the server dumped green glop in there. Wrinkling her nose slightly, Dana put the bowl on her tray and moved down to the bread bin. She searched through it until she found one that didn't have weevils all over it. *Can't they give us something edible?* Noticing that an officer watched her closely, Dana scooted down to the beverage table and picked up a glass of water that was mostly clear.

She found Elsie and Sanders and took her place beside them. They immediately dug into their food, thankful to just have something to eat. Few words filled the spaces between their chewing.

Once finished, Dana put her dishes away and noticed

George heading out. Fingering the watch in her packet, she knew what she had to do. Pushing her way past people, Dana caught up with George. She grabbed him and pulled him outside, away from the officers that always lined the area.

"I got payment," she said. "Now where is the underground?"

"It isn't that easy," said George.

"Then make it that easy." Dana stared at George with determination. She needed medicine and she needed it now.

"Look," said George. "They keep their location secret for a reason. The council is always trying to close them down."

"You said that if I got payment, then you would take me to the underground market. I held up my end."

George rubbed his face, clearly not liking the situation. He thought Dana would never be able to find the money necessary to pay for what she wanted.

"Fine," he relented. "Meet me at my place at midnight. I know you know where it is and I know you know how to get there without being noticed. And come alone."

George walked away. Midnight, that was four hours away.

Dana slowly walked back to the barracks and her bunk. She nestled in it, not bothering to get undressed since she would be having to leave in a few hours.

"Hey, what happened to you?" said Elsie.

"Oh, just tired," said Dana.

"You're sneaking out again, aren't you?" Elsie noted that Dana had not undressed.

"Keep your voice down," hissed Dana.

Elsie and Sanders both moved closer, making certain no one listened. "Where are you going?"

"I have to get something for a friend," said Dana. "I don't want to discuss it."

"What something?" pushed Elsie.

"Medicine," whispered Dana. "You know that red-headed girl that wanders around here? Well, her Nana is sick and I am going to go get some medicine for her."

"Why?"

"Because no one else will."

"We're coming too," said Sanders.

"No." Dana's voice was a bit louder than she had wanted. "Look, George said to come alone. I barely earned enough of his trust for him to take me there anyway. I don't want to lose it because I dragged along a couple of friends. He's very secretive."

Elsie and Sanders exchanged looks, not liking the entire idea.

"Fine, but you better make sure that you are back before morning, or you know what will happen," said Elsie.

"And don't accept their first price. Some of the vendors there have marked up their prices because they know that people are desperate. Haggle them down."

"Thanks," said Dana, pulling her blanket up as the lights turned off.

Luckily, Dana was able to see the clock that hung in the room. Just before midnight, Dana threw off the covers and slipped on her boots. She crawled through the same hole in the wall that Jesse had shown her earlier. Careful to avoid the beams of light that flickered from the towers, Dana clung to the shadows, hugging the exteriors of buildings as she ran through the plant.

She found the same spot in the fence that she and Jesse had crawled through before. Carefully, Dana removed the wires and slipped through to the other side. Glancing about, she ran for the small grouping of shacks where those cursed to be born in Waste Management lived. The streets remained empty. Dana wasn't surprised. Why would anyone be out at this time?

She easily remembered exactly where George's hut was. Dana knocked on the door. It opened immediately. George's meaty hand snatched her arm and yanked her inside.

"Anyone follow you?" he demanded.

"No," said Dana.

George did a quick peek outside before relaxing. He doused the lamp in the room and grabbed his jacket.

"Let's go."

Slipping outside, Dana followed George as they dashed through the alleys of Shackville. Despite being much older than Dana, George moved swiftly, avoiding any officers they came upon, while Dana struggled to keep up.

Eventually, they reached the train yard. George found a self-propelled flatcar and told Dana to get on. Together, they worked the mechanism, moving the car down the tracks toward the lights of the city.

"Here," said George as they slowed down.

Dana jumped off the cart and followed after George as he led her through back alleys of the outer edges of the city. A couple of officers patrolled by. Quickly, George snatched Dana's arm and yanked her out of the lamp light. They huddled together scrunched against a wall as they waited. Once the officers had passed, Dana and George dashed across the darkened street.

They darted down another alley until they came to what

appeared to be an apartment complex. It was more of an abandoned warehouse turned into apartments that the government had deemed fit for the average person to live, but not for its policymakers. People lived in them rent-free, but they lacked heat and air conditioning. On most days, they didn't even have electricity.

George looked down both ends of the alley, making certain no one watched them. He opened a rotted, wooden door and motioned Dana inside. A dim light bulb illuminated the steps before her, leading downward.

George marched down them. Dana followed, clutching the watch that Kenny had given her. They stomped down the hollow wooden stairs until they reached a metal door at the bottom that was bolted from the other side.

George rapped three times, paused two seconds, and then knocked another three times before ending with a succession of four quick taps. A small panel slid open, revealing two eyes.

"Silent is the night," said the man on the other side in a harsh voice.

"Where stands Lady Liberty," replied George.

"Who's she?" demanded the man, indicating Dana.

"A friend," said George.

The panel slid shut. The clicking and clacking of bolts on the other side filled the area. Slowly, the metal door pulled open. The husky man waved them in before closing it.

The place amazed Dana. It was an underground marketplace. Little shops and vendors lay everywhere as people bustled about buying and selling. Strings of incandescent light bulbs filled the ceiling, providing enough light to make one think it was sunset. Dana observed the women with their children hurrying from shop to shop with their basket of goods.

"You can't just bring anyone," said the man to George. "The bureaucrats have been cracking down on us."

"She needs stuff just like everyone else," replied George. "Stuff she can't find anywhere else."

Dana noticed an officer stroll by with a handful of items. At first, panic rose up within her until she realized that he was a customer and others walked by him unafraid.

"What is an officer doing here?" she asked.

The man at the door laughed. "You think you're the only ones who buy from the black market? We pay many officers to leave us alone. A lot of them come here for items that they are denied above."

It had never occurred to Dana that even the officers would be denied stuff. But, like her, they did not choose their career. A board chose for them.

"Come on," said George. He led Dana away to the maze of shops. "What sort of medicine do you need?"

"Something that can cure tuberculosis," replied Dana.

George rubbed his whiskers. "That's a tall order. There's only one man I know who might have that stuff. Mind you, it won't be cheap."

He led her through some aisles and past many areas of goods and wares Dana had never seen. A bakery rested on a corner, and next to it was a tailor.

"Fresh vegetables!" yelled one man from his place of business.

Dana paused momentarily. She examined the mounds of carrots, cabbage, and turnips. A bright red tomato caught her attention. It had been months since she saw one.

"Care for a few tomatoes?" asked the man. "Only six coins."

"Coins?" asked Dana.

The man laughed. "First-timer, huh? You have to get coins from the bank." He pointed at a big window with the word "bank" on it. "You take them the items you brought from outside and they exchange them for coins. Those coins are only good here though."

"Maybe later," said George, grabbing Dana's arm. "We have prior business."

Dana allowed herself to be carted away. "Why didn't you tell me about the exchange?"

"Forgot," said George. "I'm so used to it that I didn't think about it."

They walked to the bank. The big window opened the moment they approached. "What have you got?" asked the man behind the counter.

Dana handed him the watch.

The man took it, amazed that she had such a valuable item. "Where did you get this?"

"You're better off not knowing," said Dana.

"I'm sure of that," said the man. He looked at the watch with a magnifying glass. "This is the genuine article. Most bring me fakes. How did you come by this?"

Dana didn't like being asked questions. She knew she couldn't tell him the truth, and she needed the medicine. "My work took me into the city today and I took advantage of the opportunity."

"Fair enough," said the man, "though you wouldn't be the first to steal something to sell down here."

Dana's lips pursed at being called a thief. She bit her tongue to remain silent, reminding herself of why she was there.

"Well, I'd say this is worth 500 coins." The man plopped a bag on the counter.

"A thousand," said George.

"What?" said the man.

"You said that was the genuine article. Any fake is worth 500. This is worth at least 1,000."

The man behind the counter turned purple, angered at the fact that George prevented him from cheating Dana after immediately pegging her as a newbie. "Very well. One thousand coins." He plopped another bag on the counter. "Want to count it?"

"No," said George. "I trust you."

Dana took the bags and they walked off. "That's Phil," said George. "He's a good businessman, but sometimes he gets a bit greedy. This way."

George turned a corner and they walked down a row of small vendors all yelling and shouting to anyone who listened. George ignored all of them. Dana trotted to keep up.

After a few twists and turns, George stopped in front of a small store. "Here," he said.

Dana followed him inside, ignoring the grime on the window.

"May I help you?" asked the man inside.

"Hey, Bob," said George.

"Oh, hello, George. What can I do for you?"

"The little lady here needs some stuff for curing tuberculosis."

Bob peered over his reading glasses at Dana. "Really? That isn't easy to come by."

"Yes, but I told her you've got it."

"Well, let me see." Bob walked to the back and pulled out a case. He opened it and revealed five glass vials with a clear serum in them. "Got some here, but not much. How sick is the patient?"

"Very," said Dana.

"Hmmm," said the man. He grabbed two bottles. "Got any needles?"

Dana shook her head. "No."

Bob scooped up five needles, each individually wrapped in sterile packs. As he placed them all on the counter, Dana noticed him take a quick glance at the bags of coins in her arms. She scolded herself for not taking the precaution of concealing them.

"Eight hundred coins," said Bob.

Even though she was new to this, Dana knew the price was too high. "Three hundred."

Bob's eyes widened a bit. "Seven hundred."

"Three fifty."

"Five hundred," said Bob. "That's my final offer."

"You and I both know that the entire case is not even worth that much. My offer stands at 350." Dana gambled that she had guessed right. Her risk paid off. Bob's face betrayed the fact that she was right, that he had severely marked up the price thinking he could get away with it.

"Four," said Bob.

"Done," replied Dana.

George stood silent, watching the proceedings with interest. He hadn't expected Dana to know how to bargain. "We got ourselves a shrewd businessman here."

Dana handed over the coins while Bob put the items in a bag and gave it to her. "Nice doing business with you," he said. "Do you know how to inject it?"

Dana stopped cold. She hadn't thought about that.

Bob waved her back. He took out a needle he used just for such purposes.

"She will need five injections total spaced three hours apart. You will fill the needle like this. Push out any air bubbles. Then inject it in the vein, here."

Dana watched carefully as Bob demonstrated how to administer the medicine.

"You got all that?"

"Yes," said Dana.

"Alright, off you go, you haggler."

Dana didn't know if Bob was teasing or not. She left the shop with George, and they moseyed down a lane past more vendors.

"Is everyone here trying get everyone's money?" asked Dana.

George laughed. "Naw, most folk are honest. Bob was just testing you. You have "newbie" written all over you. But medicine is hard to come by, so it gets expensive. It'll take him five months to get some more."

"Fresh milk!"

Dana paused by a man holding up bottles of milk.

"Want some milk?" asked the man.

"Where did you get it?" The question popped out of her mouth before she could stop it.

The man cackled heartily. "Right here." He pointed at a dairy cow that he had down there. It looked at her while chewing on some grass. "Have to keep her down here; otherwise, them officers will take her away."

"So you just milk her and place it in the bottles?"

"That's the general idea. I told you it's fresh milk. Oh, don't worry, it won't kill you, and the bottles are sterilized. Here."

The man walked over to the cow and placed a bucket underneath the udder. Gently, he talked to her and caressed the udders so that she wouldn't jump. After squeezing enough for a glassful, he brought the bucket over and poured it into a cup.

"Drink up," he held it out to Dana.

"But won't raw milk kill you?" She had always been told that eating anything raw was bad for her health. Of course, such advice always came from helpful government officials.

"Life will kill you," laughed the man. "One day. Here, I'll try it with you."

He put some into another cup and drank it.

Unsure about it, Dana took a drink. Surprisingly, it tasted really good. "Not bad."

"Told, ya. Ten coins a bottle. And it ain't watered down like that stuff you get up top. Nor does it have manure in it."

"Manure?"

"Ever see brown stuff settling on the bottom of the milk you get up there?"

Dana thought about it and remembered that that sometimes happened. "Yes."

"That is manure," said the man. "Regulations allow for a certain amount of it. And even though they cook the milk before distributing it, manure is still manure, even when cooked."

Suddenly, Dana felt sick, realizing that she had grown up with the government approved stuff. "I'll take two bottles."

The man gladly wrapped them and handed them to her in exchange for the coins. "You'll need a bag for all that stuff," he said handing her a basket.

"Thank you."

"Come again."

"So you like shopping here?" asked George when Dana rejoined him.

Before returning to the surface, Dana decided to stop by the vegetable vendor and the bakery. She picked up a few loaves of bread and enough vegetables for a week. Jesse would need more than the medicine for her Nana.

Two hours later, Dana and George arrived back in Shackville. They parted at his hut. "Now don't tell anyone about that place. Though many use it for their own purposes, the council has many spies. They want to shut it down."

"I won't," said Dana.

"At least clear it with me first," said George.

"Okay."

He shut his door, leaving Dana alone with her bundles. Quickly, she took off down the dusty road towards Jesse's place. A single flame shone in the murky window.

Dana knocked softly on the door. "Jesse, it's Dana."

The door opened a crack, revealing Jesse's freckled face and tangled red hair. Dana went in and bolted the door. She gave the food to Jesse, whose eyes opened wide at seeing so much that was actually fit to eat.

"These are for you and your Nana," said Dana. "They should last you the week. Maybe more."

Jesse hugged Dana tightly. She returned the embrace.

Once the food had been put away, Dana pulled out the needles and vials of medicine. She called Jesse over and showed her how to administer the serum, hoping that she remembered correctly. Nana grumbled some as Dana injected the serum, but remained asleep.

"Remember, she gets four more injections, but they each have to be spaced three hours apart."

"I'll remember," said Jesse. "Will it make Nana better?"

"I hope so, sweetie." Dana's heart ached for the girl as she remembered the losses she had suffered.

Once again, dawn peeked over the horizon and Dana had to go. "I'll be back as soon as I can," she said to Jesse as she left.

Before the sun appeared completely, Dana raced back to the hole in the barbed wire fence and squeezed through. She crept back to the barracks, avoiding the patrolling officers, and closed up the hole just as the buzzer sounded.

Great, thought Dana, another day of no sleep.

CHAPTER EIGHT

Dana pushed the cart of plastic scraps across the plant. She strained against the heavy cart as she shoved it to the recycling part of the facility. Tired, she paused a moment to catch her breath.

"Well, well, well," said a familiar voice, "if it isn't the girl who broke my nose."

"Leave me alone," said Dana.

"Elsie isn't here to save you this time."

Mad Dog nodded at his friends. At once, they grabbed the cart and tipped it over, spilling its contents. Plastic bottles and sheets scattered everywhere, clinking against each other as they rolled across the ground.

"Guess you're going to be late with that stuff," sneered Mad Dog.

Infuriated from his constant taunts, Dana rushed him. She plowed into him, punching him in the jaw.

Mad Dog wiped drops of blood from his lip. "So you want to play?"

He attacked, catching Dana in the stomach. Doubled over, she head-butted him. Before the fight could go much further, whistles sounded from all over as officers ran to them, pulling them apart.

"So, you want to fight?" said Officer Burroughs, eyeing the two of them as they struggled against being held. "Very well. Summon everyone to the pit."

The buzzer sounded two consecutive times. Instantly, people dropped their tools and filed over to the gathering area. Officer Burroughs smiled maliciously as both Dana and Mad Dog were dragged over to it.

The pit was a giant hole in the middle of the plant. The only way out was by rope. Fear filled Dana as she realized what was about to happen. As the two officers hauled her closer to the edge, she put her feet out, pushing with all of her strength.

"None of that now," said one of the officers.

Dana locked eyes with George for a moment. The worried expression on his face told her all she needed to know.

"Silence, all of you," bellowed Officer Burroughs. "It seems we have ourselves a feud. What do we with do with that? Send them here."

Claps and cheers sounded from many of the officers that had crowded around as well.

"Here, you both will fight to the death. Throw them in." Officer Burroughs flicked his hand.

Dana's stomach lurched as the officer tossed her into the pit. She landed on the steep side and rolled to the bottom.

Dazed, Dana remained on the ground. A great weight landed on top of her, causing her back to ache.

Shoving Mad Dog off, Dana hopped to her feet. She watched as Mad Dog rose to his feet, staring at her with murderous eyes. Shouts filled the expanse as people took bets on who would win. Dana eyed the crowd. She soon regretted doing so as Mad Dog rammed into her, knocking her flat.

Dana seized his shoulders and flipped him over her. His moan told her she had done some damage. Dana rolled onto her hands and knees. Mad Dog charged again. She sprang to her feet and met his attack. They locked arms, each trying to deal a blow. Finally, Dana stomped on his foot. Hopping, Mad Dog released his grip on her. Dana punched him in the face, causing him to stagger back.

Dust flew into Dana's eyes as Mad Dog kicked at the dirt. Blinded, she rubbed her eyes, trying to clear them. A weight slammed into her as Mad Dog attacked. Sharp pain seized her stomach as he kicked her. Dana doubled over again, gasping for air. Immediately, a force rocked her face as Mad Dog planted his fist into it. He punched her again.

Somewhere in the distance, Dana thought she heard Elsie. Ears ringing from the force of Mad Dog's punches, Dana wobbled on her feet, shaking her head. Movement caught her eye, her vision finally clearing. She stepped into Mad Dog's attack, twisted around, and elbowed him in the stomach. She whirled around again. Facing him, Dana grasped his shoulders and pushed him downward as she rammed her knee into his face.

Jeers shot from the overexcited crowd. Many of the officers joined the commotion, yelling at them and telling them what to do. Some exchanged coins from lost bets.

Dana turned back to Mad Dog. He charged her again. She sidestepped. Mad Dog had read her movements and moved to the side as well, catching her off guard. He flung her to the ground. Before Dana could regain her feet, Mad Dog kicked her repeatedly.

Sore and confused, Dana remained in the dirt. Mad Dog reached down and picked up a rock. He lifted it high above his head just as Dana rolled onto her back. She knew what was coming.

"Go ahead," said Dana.

Mad Dog started to throw the rock, but stopped. He looked into Dana's eyes and the mixture of defiance and acceptance within them. Not a bit of fear filled her.

Having never killed anyone before, Mad Dog didn't know what to do. He scanned the crowd and their excitement. Disgust filled him. Refusing to play their game, he dropped the rock.

Enraged at his entertainment being foiled, Officer Burroughs stepped to the front of the crowd. "Kill her," he yelled at Mad Dog.

Neither Mad Dog, nor Dana moved.

"Shoot them both," said Officer Burroughs.

"Wait!" George pushed his way through the crowd. "Leave them be."

"You dare challenge me?"

"You've had your fun. What is the point in killing them?"

"What indeed?" Officer Burroughs studied George, Dana, and Mad Dog. "Get them out of there! Everyone get back to work!"

Before George knew what had happened, Officer Burroughs struck him with a baton, forcing him to his knees. Not satisfied, he hit George three more times with the baton.

As he raised his club a fifth time, a hand seized it. Mad Dog, who had scrambled out of the pit first, held it tightly. His eyes said what words could never convey.

Officer Burroughs relaxed his arm. As Mad Dog released his grip, Officer Burroughs swung his baton at him, smacking him in the neck and leaving a bloody stripe. Mad Dog crumpled to the ground. "When I tell you to kill someone, filth, you do it."

Clinging to the rope and the edge of the pit, Dana watched the whole thing. She heaved her way onto solid ground and ran to George. Elsie and Sanders ran to him as well.

Mad Dog's friends reached his side. They inspected his wound and determined it wasn't life threatening.

Elsie encouraged Dana to lean on her shoulder while Sanders helped George up. They all left the area in silence.

~ ~ ~

The train moved swiftly along the railroad tracks at 250 mph. President Klens barely noticed it. Her luxurious train moved so smoothly, it was as though she were actually in her own bed on a calm night. She settled in a plush, soft chair, placing her feet on the footrest and looking forward to being in her accommodations when she arrived at the eastern capital. Though they had done their best to make her train comfortable, she still ended up with a few aches and pains.

Oh, the rigors of traveling, thought the president. She

wished she didn't have to make these constant trips to show the people that she cared. The truth was, she didn't.

"What is on the agenda after we arrive?" asked President Klens.

"You are to visit the agricultural sector," said Williams, her secretary. "After that, it is off to the Waste Management plant."

President Klens groaned. She hated going to these places. Her secretary insisted on it as a way to convince the people that she actually felt affection toward them. Her father never liked it either, but went along with it. It kept the masses from rebelling. *If it was good enough for him, then it should be for me.*

The odorous stench of those places always made her stomach sick. And the grime, she thought to herself. Last time, she had gotten one of her $500 shoes coated in muck. She couldn't bear to wear them after that and had them thrown away.

"Is it cold there this time of year?" she asked.

"No, ma'am," said Williams. "It is still tolerable this time of year."

"When will we return to the Los Angeles Basin?"

"In about two weeks."

President Klens wished it were sooner. The weather never changed there and was always warm. And her mansion was there. She looked out the window and the world that whizzed past. "Such a waste."

Williams glanced out the window at what had been dubbed the Wasteland. Waste or not, she thought, there was no living thing out here. "Yes, ma'am," he said, his philosophy to always humor the president.

"Is there any chance that we can harness the potential of this area?"

"I don't know, ma'am, except for oil," replied Williams. "It is truly a barren wasteland. Only sand. Nothing grows out here, and no one tries to live out here, except thieves and bandits."

"Just as well. Let them rot out there."

"Anyway, it isn't as though we need this arid place," said Williams. "The southern region of the east provides what food we need. They even produce the cigars you are so fond of. The northern region gives us our coal. The northwest provides what lumber we need, and Waste Management takes care of the garbage."

"How true. But I am not so sure of things like you are."

"Yes, ma'am."

"Well, hurry up and get this train where we need to go," said President Klens. "The sooner I get this PR mission over with, the sooner I can return to my home and the people that truly matter."

"Don't forget, you are also to meet with Seth Michaels."

"Who is he?"

"The First Councilman of the Eastern Region. He has a few ideas that might be of use to you. I suggest placating the man."

"Very well."

President Klens moved from her plush chair to a couch with a silk lining. The chair was too lumpy for her taste. Perhaps the couch would be better.

~~~

Dana moseyed around outside in the dark, along the edges of the perimeter around the Waste Management plant. A month had passed since she had first arrived. It felt more like a year.

They had been allowed some extra free time and were even permitted to wander outside, as long as they did not go beyond the boundary. She eyed the barbed wire fence that encompassed the area. Guard towers were stationed at various points, with two officers in each.

She looked out at the fields beyond, longing to go there. Memories of picking wild strawberries with her grandfather flittered through her mind. She missed those days and the innocence they held.

Dana studied the barbed wire fence and its eight feet of sharp metal barbs. They had been told that all this was for their safety. Dana felt more like a prisoner.

The whistle of a train stole her attention. She glanced at the streamlined, luxury train as it pulled into its station. So the rumors were true, thought Dana. President Klens is coming for a visit.

Mad Dog walked by. He stopped momentarily and stared at her before moving on. He had not talked to her since the fight. Dana felt as if she could die at any moment from one of his stares.

Well, tomorrow is another day, she thought to herself.

The buzzer sounded, indicating that their free time was over. Dana slowly walked over to the barracks. A thought entered her mind, something she had not thought about for a long time. *What was Kenny up to?*

Once again Dana and George worked side by side at the incinerator. They methodically raked the garbage into the flames below them. Neither said a word. Neither wanted to, as they tired from their work. Elsie and Sanders had also been assigned to the incinerator that day. Dana looked over and smiled at her friend.

The heat from the fires seared her skin, but she had noticed that it began to toughen up. A strand of hair fell in her face. Dana brushed it aside. She scraped more refuse into the flames. Blisters formed on the heels of her hands from the continued use of the rake and the holes that developed in the gloves.

An agonizing wail filled the area, halting everyone. Looking up, Dana saw that Tony, one of Mad Dog's friends, had his arm caught in the grinders. No one moved to help him as he hung there with his bloodied arm caught between the gears.

Angered at people's apathy, Dana ran for Tony. She snatched a ladder and placed it under him to stand on. Grateful, Tony did so relieving the weight from his arm.

Carefully, Dana climbed the gears of the grinder, which had frozen in place. She hoped they wouldn't move or she, too, would be caught. The blood and bits of meat entangled in the gears sickened her. Swallowing back vomit, Dana concentrated on what she had come to do.

"My arm!" cried Tony.

"Look away," said Dana.

Tony did so as tears filled his eyes from the pain.

Dana studied the situation and realized that there was nothing she could do, except yank what was left of his arm out of there. She knew there would be no saving it.

"I am going to pull it out, but it's going to hurt. Bad," said Dana. "When I do, we both need to jump back fast or we will get sucked into this thing when it starts up again."

Tony nodded his head in understanding.

Dana knew that all eyes watched her. She had no doubts that the officers were taking bets again about her chances of success.

Dana wrapped her hands around Tony's arm and yanked.

His agonizing screams filled the area, echoing around all of them. The moment his arm was freed, the gears of the grinder started up. Dana pushed them both away. A moment of weightlessness took hold before they crashed to the black dirt.

Dana breathed deeply, recovering from having the wind being knocked out of her. Tony's groans and grunts brought her back to the task at hand. He cradled his mangled arm. Quickly, Dana took her bandana and wrapped it around Tony's bleeding limb to stem the flow of blood.

Officer Burroughs barreled his way through the gathering crowd. "What's going on here? Why have you stopped work?"

"There was an accident," said one man.

"Accident?" demanded Officer Burroughs.

"This man needs a hospital," said Dana, holding Tony up. Her authoritative tone did not go unnoticed by those around her.

"Does he now?" Officer Burroughs snatched Tony's mangled arm, twisting and turning it as he studied it. Pain filled Tony's face as he tried to not cry out.

"This arm is beyond saving," said Officer Burroughs. "What is a man with one arm supposed to do in this place? What use is a man with one arm?"

Officer Burroughs circled around Tony as he addressed the people around him. Dana did not like the direction his speech took.

"We only have so many resources at our disposal. Should we waste them on him?" Officer Burroughs pointed his baton at Tony. "So I ask you again, what do we do with a one-armed man when his usefulness has been used up?"

Without warning, Officer Burroughs seized Tony by the shoulders and threw him into the hole that led straight to the incinerator and the fires below. Tony's scream echoed on the way down until it came to an abrupt end. No one moved, too scared to challenge him.

"That is what we do with those who are of no more use to us," said Officer Burroughs.

Infuriated, Dana charged him. She punched him in the face. "You jerk! There was no reason for that!"

With expert skill, Officer Burroughs flung her off him, throwing her to the ground. He smacked her with his baton. "It's time that you learn your place," he snarled as he raised his baton again.

George stepped forward. "I think she has learned her lesson."

Officer Burroughs slowly lowered his weapon. He eyed George a moment as his anger dissipated. "See to it that she has," he said. "All of you, get back to work!"

Elsie ran for Dana. "Are you alright?" She pulled off her bandana and dabbed the bruised cut that formed on Dana's cheek.

"You need to be careful," said George, holding his hand out to her.

Dana took it as he helped her up. She glanced at Mad Dog, who remained, still staring at the hole that led to the incinerator. The shock on his face said it all. Not only had he never seen someone die before, but he had also never lost someone he cared about. The two locked eyes for a moment before Dana turned away and returned to work.

The same officer that had taunted Dana earlier for trying to save a man's life from certain death in the incinerator strolled by. Angered, she glared at him. "Did you win your bet?" she spat, not caring if her rudeness cost her.

He stopped, looked at her, and continued on without a word.

CHAPTER NINE

The next day, Dana awoke like everyone else and put on her clothes, ready to work in the Waste Management plant for another day. She ambled into the eating hall with everyone else, wishing for more sleep. The clinking and clanking of spoons barely registered. She shuffled through the line with the rest. More glop. This time it was red. She didn't want to know what was in it.

As Dana sat with Elsie and Sanders, an extra slice of bread appeared on her tray. Curious, Dana looked up. Mad Dog stood there, holding his tray. He never said anything, but Dana understood the message. It was for Tony.

She smiled in appreciation. Words were not needed, as they had come to an understanding.

"Morning all," said George as he sat down.

Dana noticed a slip of paper with the insignia of an

eagle on it. She reached for it for a closer look, but George snatched it and buried it in his pocket.

"What…"

"Nothing," said George in a tone that indicated he did not want to talk about it.

Dana let it drop. Whatever he was involved in was none of her affair.

"Listen up!" yelled Officer Burroughs.

Silence fell upon the room.

"I have two very important announcements," continued Officer Burroughs, "First, we need people to go to the agricultural district to pick up their discarded material. George Saule, Dana Ginary, and Lionel Hoffman, you just volunteered. Second, the president will be visiting later this week. I am certain you will all wear your best attire and show her the respect due. Remember your position and we will have no discourse."

Dana groaned. She had never volunteered to pick up more garbage, but "volunteer" was a meaningless word in her world. She also did not look forward to meeting the president. Dana didn't know much about the woman, but figured she was just like everyone else who held a position of power.

"That is all for now," said Officer Burroughs as he snapped his electronic pad off and left.

"Saule, Ginary," said an officer. "Let's go. You have your assignments."

Dana looked down at her half-eaten breakfast. *Looks like I go hungry again.* She pushed her bowl to Sanders, while George gave his to Elsie. Someone should at least be able to eat it.

Together, they stood up and walked to where Lionel—Dana had never met him—stood waiting with another officer. The two officers led them to a truck parked just outside. A hint of a chill rested in the air, informing Dana that summer was ending and winter was coming.

"In," ordered the officer, pointing to the back of the truck.

They obliged. Five officers waited for them inside, each armed with guns. Dana sat on a seat that felt like it had been made out of sharp rocks and concrete. A huge jolt bounced her as the truck sped forward. Her head ached from the movement.

Jerking side to side, Dana's stomach felt queasy as she vainly tried to hold down her meager breakfast. Unable to hold it any longer, she turned away from the others and vomited. Feeling better, Dana took her seat again. No one looked at her. She guessed they had seen it all before.

Dana peeked through the small opening in the canvas roof of the truck. They had left the city and entered a more rural area. She had never been to the Agricultural District, but knew that it lay away from any signs of civilization. Those within the Agricultural District were even more removed from society than the ones in Waste Management.

Tall fences with spikes on them appeared. Dana looked at the deadly fences. Guard towers swung past the truck.

"George…" Dana began.

George put his finger over his mouth, telling her to keep quiet.

"No talking," barked one of the officers.

Dana sat back in her seat. *Why is everyone on edge?* She didn't understand the change in their demeanor, but knew something was terribly wrong.

The truck rolled over a huge bump in the road, causing

Dana to bump her head on the ceiling. She rubbed the sore spot. Suddenly, she pitched toward the front of the truck as it stopped abruptly. Righting herself, Dana wished she could leave.

The back of the truck opened up, allowing sunlight to spill inside. The officers jumped out first.

"Out! Now!"

Cautiously, Dana and the others hopped out of the truck. They lined up next to it. Armed officers stood everywhere. The place was more of a prison than Waste Management.

Ragged people stood everywhere. In open fields were men, women, and children. They dug holes for planting, raked, and watered. Ladders nestled beside each tree in the orchard as people stood upon them, picking apples and dropping them into a basket. One man put an apple in his pocket.

"Hey, you!" yelled an officer. "What do you think you're doing?" He yanked the man off the ladder and beat him repeatedly with the butt of his weapon. Once finished, he walked off. Those watching did nothing, turning back to their work.

"That is what happens when you steal from the people," said a uniformed man. "My name is Officer Verikruse. I run this establishment. You three must be from Waste Management."

Dana, George, and Lionel remained silent.

Officer Verikruse continued. "Normally, we do not have our dumpsters emptied so soon, but with the president's arrival, we must make a good impression." He flicked his hand. Another officer ran over. "Take them to the dumpsters. See to it that they are quick."

"Stealing from the people?" said Dana. She bit her tongue, wishing she could take back her comment.

"Pardon?" said Officer Verikruse.

"You said that that man was stealing from the people, but he probably worked to keep the tree alive and then harvests the fruit when it is ready."

"What is your point?"

"Well, isn't he people?"

Officer Verikruse roared with laughter. "He is a laborer. Sent here because the career board felt his talents would be of use here. But these crops belong to the people of Dystopia. If anyone takes more than his allotment, then he is stealing."

Dana looked around at the half-starved laborers toiling in the fields. Many wore forlorn expressions. Whatever hope they had, whatever dreams they had, had died.

"This way," said the officer that led them to the dumpsters.

On the far side of the district were 10 huge dumpsters, each overflowing. Dana gagged on the stench.

"Just ignore it," said George.

Choking, Dana breathed through her mouth, hoping that it would reduce the effect of the smell. It didn't.

Together, the three pushed the dumpsters one at a time to the lift. Dana's muscles strained from the effort. The heavy dumpsters screeched and squealed as they pushed, their wheels refusing to turn.

Once on the lift, George jumped into the control room. He worked the lift, heaving each dumpster up and emptying their contents in the waiting dump truck. The deafening noise hurt Dana's ears, despite her efforts at covering them.

Armed guards watched all of their movements. The hairs on the back of Dana's neck prickled the longer their job took. She wanted to leave.

After the final dumpster had been emptied, George set it down carefully and shut off the machine. "She's all ready!"

The driver of the dump truck waved, started the engine, and took off.

The armed officers escorted them back to where the truck that had brought them waited. Dana watched as people worked tirelessly to produce the food that fed the cities of Dystopia.

"Come on!" yelled a man with a whip.

Five men strained to turn a wheel that worked the irrigation system which watered the fields. Momentarily, Dana wondered why they didn't use a modernized system. Then, she understood why. With the amount of people living there, the officers needed work for them to do. Men took the place of machines.

"Hurry up!" yelled another officer at her.

Dana stopped dawdling and sprinted forward.

Shouts and yells rose up. Stopping, Dana turned to see what the commotion was. A man had dropped his bag of brussel sprouts and ran for the fence. He came straight for Dana, heading for the spiked fence. An officer pulled out his rifle, aimed, and fired. The single shot filled the area, echoing off the trees and surrounding hills.

The fleeing man paused from being hit in the back. Staggering, he took a few more steps before collapsing. Instinctively, Dana caught the man. His vacant eyes stared back at her as he died in her arms, blood pouring from his wound.

Gently, Dana laid the man on the grass. She closed his eyes, unsure of what else to do. Dana surveyed the faces around her. The laborers all turned back to their duties, except for one woman. She must have known him, thought Dana.

It seemed cold to leave his body there, so Dana folded his hands on his chest. Despite the eyes that watched her, she peeled off her jacket and covered the body.

George's hand wrapped around her arm. "Dana, come on."

Dana didn't move. How could she?

"Dana." George hauled her to her feet and dragged her to the truck. They walked past the officers that watched them. Despite her better sense, Dana glanced back at the man that had died before her. Two officers tossed her jacket aside and carted his corpse away, allowing his feet to leave tracks in the mud.

"One day," said Officer Verikruse to Dana, "you will all learn that there is no escape from this."

Dana gawked at him. She started to open her mouth, but George pushed her into the truck, cutting her off. He and Lionel hopped in behind her.

The diesel engine of the truck roared to life. A sharp lurch told her that they had moved on, going back to her life as a waste-rat.

CHAPTER TEN

Officer Burroughs licked his lips as he brought the raspberry turnover to his salivating mouth. His mind already raced with the satisfying taste of the sugar and flaky pastry. The door to his office burst open. Immediately, Officer Burroughs dropped his turnover and shoved the plate aside, hoping that the intruder did not notice and that the stack of books on his desk hid the forbidden treat.

"What is the meaning of this?" demanded Officer Burroughs. He cut himself off when he noticed the uniform on the man that entered his domain.

The well-built man before him wore the navy blue uniform and yellow sash of one well above Officer Burroughs' station. He carried a switch in his leather gloved hands.

"I will ignore your rudeness," said the man, taking off his hat. Every inch of his uniform reflected the light.

"I'm sorry. I... I... didn't..." stammered Officer Burroughs.

"My name is Colonel Fernau," the man said as he paced the room. He picked at an item on a shelf with his stick, frowned, and flicked it to the floor. "I am here on an important matter."

"Colonel Fernau?" Officer Burroughs vainly tried to grasp what was happening.

"Perhaps you haven't heard of me," said Colonel Fernau. "Suffice it to say that I am here on orders of our First Councilman."

"But why here? We are only Waste Management."

"You are only Waste Management," snapped Colonel Fernau, "I am here to keep the peace and to keep order. As you are probably aware, there has been a resistance movement growing in Dystopia. Shocking, I know. But there are those who do not desire our ordered world of peace and equality."

"Well, yes," said Officer Burroughs, pushing the plate further into the shadows of the books. "But what does that have to do with me?"

"Because many of the members of the resistance are believed to be here."

Officer Burroughs gulped. This did not bode well for him. "I know that there is an underground…"

"Oh, I don't give a damn about the underground market!" Colonel Fernau swatted a chair with his stick. "I want the leaders of the resistance. They always manage to slip through our grasp. They always manage to replace their members or protect their leaders. And their movement is growing. Something the First Councilman and president will not allow.

"They are terrorists whose only goal is to destroy us with their misguided notion of individual liberty. Liberty. What a laughable concept. Freedom is the desire of selfish men who care only for themselves and not their fellow man.

"No, you idiotic dolt. I want the leaders of the resistance. I know many of them are here. I have traced them here. And you will find them for me. Once found, everything else they've created will crumble, including their precious underground market."

"Find? How?" asked Officer Burroughs, not liking at all where this conversation went.

"You spy on your own people, do you not?"

"Well, yes."

"Then watch. Observe. Anyone who is difficult to control is suspect. Anyone who stands out from the crowd. Find them and bring them to me."

Colonel Fernau used his stick to drag the plate with the turnover into the light. "Or perhaps you do not want to?"

Officer Burroughs licked his lips. He knew he was in trouble. "I'll find them. Anyone who is suspicious will be sent to your…"

"They will be sent to the Detention Center. That is where I am located."

"Yes, sir." Officer Burroughs rose from his chair and saluted.

"By the way, the president will be here within a day or two. See to it that there are no incidents."

"Yes, sir."

"And," Colonel Fernau picked up the raspberry turnover, "I will dispose of this contraband item for you."

The colonel marched out the door, letting it slam behind him. He handed the turnover to one of his officers. "Get rid of this thing."

The officer took the turnover. When no one was looking, he shoved the entire dessert in his mouth.

~~~

Dana fiddled with her food as she stared into her bowl of crap surprise. That's what many within the plant called their meals.

"I'm sorry," said Elsie. "We heard what happened."

"I don't want to talk about it," said Dana. She wanted to go home, but this had become her home.

"Maybe you should," coaxed Elsie.

"I don't." Dana picked up her tray of untouched food and dumped it where all dirty trays were to go. She marched back to the barracks, wanting to be alone or with people who did not know about the day's events.

She decided to visit Jesse. Dana hadn't been back since she delivered the medicine. Even though the sun was still up, Dana decided to risk it. She crawled through the hole in the barracks and followed the path to the fence. No one paid her any attention. This was their free time, which meant the residents of Waste Management were allowed to wander a bit. Making certain no one watched her, Dana slipped through the fence and ran down the hill to Shackville. Once there, it didn't take long for her to reach Jesse's home.

"Come in, my dear," said Nana as Dana opened the door.

Jesse's face lit up. The girl jumped to her feet and squeezed Dana in a big hug. Dana returned it, finding comfort in the girl's arms. A single tear rolled down her cheek.

"What is it, dear?" asked Nana.

"Nothing," said Dana. "I just stopped by to see how you were doing."

"Much better now that I've had some medicine. I don't know how you managed to get it, but we both thank you."

"Nana is all cured," said Jesse.

Nana sensed that something bothered Dana. "Jesse, will you go over to Mrs. Hammer's for a while? Dana and I have something to discuss."

Jesse's face fell a bit. She grabbed her coat and left. "That always means that you want to talk about things that you think are too grown up for me."

"She is a smart one," said Nana as Jesse shut the door. "Now, why don't you tell me what happened. Don't deny it. I know something bothers you."

Dana settled in a chair. A heavy sigh escaped her lips as she knew that there would be no getting out of it. "Today, I was sent to the Agricultural District to pick up their garbage. A man tried to escape and was shot down like an animal. He died in my arms. No one did anything. No one ever does anything.

"People here get beaten or killed and no one does anything! Why? Why do we all just sit here and let it happen?"

Allowing Dana to release her frustrations, Nana listened patiently. "When you live in a world where evil is allowed to flourish, you get used to it."

"So people just accept it?"

"Yes, they do. We live in a world where our livelihoods are chosen for us. My great-great-grandparents said that it happened slow, but happened because people stopped caring about responsibility. They wanted to be free of it. So this is the result. Now we have lived this way for so long that we don't question it."

"Doesn't seem right."

"It's not. People in our society are never allowed to move up, but they can always move down."

"What do you mean?" asked Dana.

"Mrs. Hammer's husband once worked for the Board of Medicine. He had the radical idea that individuals be allowed to decide for themselves if they accepted a doctor's medical treatment or not. Well, that idea did not go over very well, so the Career Assignment Board gave him a new career. They sent him here.

"But you, who were sent here straight away, you will never be allowed to escape."

Dana saw Nana's point. She knew her chances of getting out of Waste Management were extremely slim.

"Now, the Agricultural District," continued Nana, "has always been a bit separate from the rest of our society. So are the coal mining operations that are allowed. Farming is not an easy business. Your harvest depends upon the amount of rain you receive. You spend long hours in the sun weeding, planting, plowing, and picking.

"It is a hard life and a short one. All farms are managed by the Food Management Board. Those who work there are not allowed to keep any of it for themselves. The people at the top get what they want, and the remainder is doled out to the rest of us."

"So why are the farms kept separate?"

"Well, it takes a lot of land to farm enough to feed a large population. But mostly, they suffer many revolts out there. It's easier to deny events if no one witnesses them. Besides, you'll find that many people may like to eat something, or use some product, but they don't want to know where it comes from.

"The trash that you are forced to incinerate each day. How many people in our society really care about where it goes once they toss it?"

"But his eyes. They..."

"I know, dear," said Nana, laying a wrinkled hand on Dana's. "I've seen the same look many times in my life. Don't let it trouble you. He made his choice. He knew that he was most likely going to get killed. And I think in the end, that was what he wanted."

"I've heard stories about people jumping into the incinerator," said Dana.

"Yes, that happens," said Nana. "Many a man can't take this life and they see no other way out. Mrs. Hammer's husband met the same fate."

"I wish things would change."

"Maybe you should join the resistance."

"What?"

Nana laughed.

"I thought you knew about them since you were able to get the medicine. And there is only one place to get it."

Jesse burst through the door, breathing heavily. "Nana, Mrs. Hammer is dead. Her face is blue and her body stiff."

Dana lowered her head. It sounded as though the woman died several days ago and nobody noticed.

"Death comes for us all in the end," replied Nana, looking directly at Dana. "Go get George."

Jesse dashed outside and returned minutes later with George. When Nana explained what had happened, his face softened some. "Come on," he said to Dana.

She followed him to Mrs. Hammer's house. The stench of death struck Dana the moment she entered the building. George acted as though he didn't notice a thing. Commanding her stomach to settle down, Dana went inside and followed George's instructions. Together, they wrapped the body in linen and carried it outside.

A crowd had already gathered. Word had spread fast about Mrs. Hammer's death. Dana glanced at them as they each carried a single, white candle.

"This way," said George as he directed Dana to a conveyer belt on the edge of Shackville. She allowed him to lead her. Respectfully, they laid Mrs. Hammer on the belt. George pushed the button that controlled it.

"Shouldn't there be some time before…"

"She's been dead for a few days," interrupted George. "No point in waiting any longer. This is as close to a funeral as anyone in this place will ever get. This belt goes straight to the incinerator. If you got any words, best say them now."

Dana stepped back into the crowd that had gathered, taking her place next to Jesse.

One by one, the candles came to life as they were lit. Their flames danced in the breeze. One man started to sing. Slowly, others followed suit.

> We gather here to say farewell
> to Mrs. Hamilton. So ring the bell;
> it's chimes shall not be quelled.

As the song ended, every one blew out their candles. One by one, people went back to their homes. Only Dana remained watching as the wrapped body of what had once been a living person moved steadily to the incinerator, and its final resting place.

"Come," said George. "Come with me."

Dana didn't argue. She walked with George back to his hut, surprised that he invited her inside. She sat in a chair wondering why he had summoned her there.

"Here." George handed her a small glass with brown liquid in it.

Dana studied it a moment before swallowing it in one gulp. Instantly, her throat burned from the liquid, causing her to cough.

"That'll put some hair on your chest," laughed George.

"What is that stuff?"

"Whiskey. Brew it myself. Not that it's legal, mind you."

Dana felt a bit dizzy from the drink.

"Want some more?"

"No." She gave the glass back to George.

"You're probably wondering why I invited you here," said George. "I don't normally allow guests, but since today was troubling, I figured you needed company."

Troubling put the day's events mildly, thought Dana.

"You never had someone die in your arms before, have you?"

"No."

"It takes something from you."

"But the man that fell in the incinerator..."

"But his death was quick. Oh, that doesn't make it any less important. But you never saw his eyes as his life left him.

You never looked in here," George pointed two fingers at his eyes. "This is where you see a man's soul. His life."

"So what do you want me to do?" asked Dana, still confused as to why George brought her to his home.

"Get over it."

Dana glared at him.

"Oh, I don't mean it like that. You're young. You got a lot to learn about life. So, I'm going to tell you something, and hopefully it will keep you from becoming one of those hollowed eyed folk at the plant. You're going to witness a lot of horrible things in this life, but you cannot let it take hold of you."

"What do you mean?" asked Dana.

"Don't let your emotions control you. When you see something bad happen, grieve for the moment, but move on. Stay in control of yourself. Because if you let it eat at you, if you let it gnaw at your spirit, then they win."

"They?"

"The very people that put you here because you were an inconvenience to them."

"But I am only one person."

"We are all just one person," said George, "but don't let that stop you from doing what you know is right.

"Like the rest of us, I'm willing to bet that you have lost people close to you to our standard of equality."

Dana nodded, remembering her sister and her grandfather.

"They do that to instill fear. To keep you contained. The death of that man is another of their methods. Don't let them control this"—George pointed at his head—"or this." He pointed at his heart. "The day you allow someone to control them is the day you become a slave."

The buzzer from the facility echoed in the distance.

"We need to get you back before they notice your absence."

"Is that how you've managed to survive here so long?" asked Dana.

George smiled. "Honey, I'm still here because I'm a cranky, middle-aged man whom the good Lord doesn't want."

George opened the door, waving Dana out. "Now I know Jesse showed you a way in and out of the plant, but I know a better one."

CHAPTER

ELEVEN

"Everyone up!"

Officers moved through the barracks, clanging their batons on the bed posts to wake everyone. Dana sat up, rubbing her eyes.

"Up!" an officer yelled at her.

Dana stood up and pulled on her clothes. They had actually been pressed and washed in the middle of the night in preparation of the president's arrival. Officer Burroughs didn't want them looking too filthy for her annual visit.

The line of people shifted over to the eating hall. Dana looked at her tray in shock at seeing a slice of ham with oatmeal. "What happened to the usual fare of slimy glop?" she asked the server.

The man glared at her, but remained silent.

Of course, thought Dana, the president is coming, so we are allowed something different and halfway decent.

Dana sat with Elsie and Sanders as had become her custom. She tried to enjoy her meal while she could, not knowing when they'd be allowed decent food again.

"She's coming today," said Sanders, referring to the president's visit.

"We never would have figured that out," replied Elsie. "What first alerted you to all this?"

Sanders gave her a piercing stare.

"Is that why we're being allowed real food?" asked someone sitting nearby.

"Yeah," said Sanders. "It's their way of letting us know that she cares about our plight. We don't even have to work today."

"Nope," said Elsie, "we just have to show up, show our respect, and the rest of the day is free."

"Free," muttered Dana.

"What's with you?" asked Elsie.

Dana stared at her plate still thinking about the man that had died in her arms, gunned down like an animal. "I'm starting to wonder how we think of ourselves as free when everything we do is regulated."

"What do you mean?" asked Sanders.

Picking at the ham on her plate, Dana looked up and looked both Elsie and Sanders in the eyes. "Yesterday, I was sent to the Agricultural District where the food is grown for us. They were treated worse there than we are here. One man tried to escape and the officers killed him. They didn't even think about it. They just shot him. He died right in front of me, and I will never forget the look on his face."

"What…"

"And one man was so hungry that he took an apple from

the bunch he had just picked. I watched as officers beat him senseless. No one did anything. Not even me."

"Well, what could you have done?" asked Elsie. "This is our world."

"Elsie's right," said Sanders. "There isn't anything you could have done. You know why we were all sent here in the first place."

"Perhaps you're right," said Dana.

The buzzer sounded. As one, people gathered up their trays and placed them in the drop-off area.

"Time to line up," said Elsie.

Dana followed the line as they marched to the main area of the plant. The machinery and incinerator had been shut off. Dana sighed. A day of no work meant tomorrow would be filled with added labor.

She took her place in the second row of the lineup. Glancing around, Dana had never realized just how many people actually lived and worked in Waste Management.

Armed officers marched into the area. They formed a protective barrier around them. More walked in front, forming groups of two near the platform that had been constructed for the president.

Instantly, the loudspeakers came to life as the anthem of Dystopia blared through them. Trumpets and strings played a triumphant, yet ominous tune.

Trying to peek over the shoulders of the person in front of her, Dana stood on her tippy toes. She watched as a lone figure silhouetted by light casually entered the room.

Officer Burroughs clapped loudly. A loud explosion sounded as applause filled the room. Dana glanced about her. Everyone put their hands together, but many did so halfheartedly. She kept hers by her side.

Men burst into song, singing the anthem of Dystopia. Dana refused to join in.

> We are the land
> of strength and unity.
> Together, we stand
> in collective serenity.
>
> One man alone;
> weak and overcome,
> he dies so easily.
>
> Together, we are strong
> with strength in numbers;
> nothing more do we need.
>
> Hail to mighty Dystopia
> where we have equality.
> Hail to mighty Dystopia
> where all live free.

After the singing ended, Officer Burroughs stepped forward and greeted President Klens. Their pasted smiles told Dana that it was all ceremony; they didn't care for one another.

A man dressed in a crisp uniform with a switch in his hands caught Dana's attention. Instantly, she feared him. His cold expression and heartless eyes filled her with dread. Dana hoped to never meet him.

"Thank you. Thank you all," said President Klens in the microphone. "And thank you, Officer Burroughs, for allowing me to visit your establishment."

"Like he had a choice," muttered the man next to Dana.

"It is an honor to visit you all here at the Waste Management plant. As you know, the job you do here is of vital importance to Dystopia. It is you who keep our society clean.

"And we are aware of your sacrifice. That is why I have decided to allow you all two days off a week. Days that you can use as you desire. And for those of you who have just been assigned here, your families will be allowed to visit for a day.

"I know the importance of family," continued President Klens, "and I know that you must miss them terribly. Unfortunately, some of us are called upon to make sacrifices. And for your efforts, you are all to be commended and honored."

President Klens paused a moment as she surveyed the crowd, wondering what affect her words had. Stoic faces stared back at her.

"Unfortunately, Dystopia has suffered a few economic reversals. Some were beyond our means to control. But most of it was because of a small group of people who do not like our ordered society. They believe that they should be able to do as they please, regardless of how it affects the rest of us. But I refuse to allow our family, our collective, to be done away with by such selfishness.

"Therefore, I have come to ask you all to once again make a sacrifice for the good of our society. I know what many of you are thinking. How can we when you have already given so much? But at a time when our resources are limited, we must all tighten our belts.

"Therefore, I am going to propose a measure where everyone, I repeat, everyone will have to use only what they need. And if they have more than they need, they are to give to someone who has less. This way, we will all prosper."

"And what sacrifices are you making?" shouted one man. Dana glanced over. He was no more than 25.

Instantly, officers pushed their way through the crowd and seized him. He kicked as they hauled him away. She never saw the man again. Never even knew his name, though now she wished she did.

Dana glanced back at President Klens. An incensed expression filled her face. She brushed back a strand of hair, the diamond bracelet on her wrist glinting in the sunlight.

"But these lean times will not last forever," continued President Klens, controlling her voice, "as one day, we will have more than enough to meet our needs. But despite this setback, there is one thing you can all be thankful for. We have achieved true equality."

"What equality?" The words were out of Dana's mouth before she realized that she had even spoken them.

"Excuse me?" said President Klens.

The crowd parted allowing Dana to be fully exposed.

"What equality?" repeated Dana. "I am certain that you have never worked a day in your life doing manual labor. Your father was the president before you, and your grandfather before him. When have you ever had to wonder if you'd have food to eat that day? And from the looks of it, I don't think your meals are rationed."

President Klens pinched her face as it flushed red with anger. She hated being challenged, especially by some young upstart. "You did not join in singing the anthem. Why?"

Dana choked a moment. *So she did notice.* "Because the words aren't true."

"Really?"

Dana saw George shake his head at her, warning her to remain silent. Dana's anger refused to let her obey. "How can you claim freedom and equality when our lives are chosen for us? Those whose parents run the various advisory boards always get the best careers, while the rest of us are sent here. They get the best of everything. Asking questions means being arrested and disappearing. And what about the children that are born here? They will never be allowed to leave this place."

"The career board uses a lottery system to pick the careers of every individual," said President Klens in a silky voice.

"Well, the lottery is fixed," replied Dana. "Why can't you just leave people alone to live their own lives?"

"She's right," said someone within the crowd.

Murmurs spread through the workers at the plant. Others started yelling. Suddenly, the place exploded as shots rang out. A few fell from the gunfire. Incensed, others grabbed what they could, preparing for a full blown riot. Dana stood her ground, not comprehending what had just happened.

"STOP!"

President Klens' voice rang out over the crowd, quieting everything. Workers dropped their glass bottles and rocks, while officers lowered their guns.

"Must we resort to violence?" said President Klens. Her calm tone frightened Dana. "So you have questions, my dear. We all do. Our society is not perfect, but it is better than what has existed in the past, where selfishness and greed reigned supreme as everyone looked only to their needs, whilst forgetting about the common good.

"But to show you that I am fair and open-minded, I will let all this be forgotten. You will retain the days off that I have decreed you shall have, and your families will still be allowed to visit. And as an added measure, I will see to it personally that your food is of the highest quality."

Deafening silence wafted over them as President Klens whispered something to the uniformed man Dana did not like. Hurriedly, she walked outside and away from an impending riot.

"Back to your barracks!" yelled Officer Burroughs.

The officers raised their guns. Knowing when not to argue, people filed back to their barracks. Dana fell in line, wondering what she had just unleashed.

~~~

"That little bitch!" fumed President Klens, referring to Dana. "How dare she challenge me!"

"There is a growing sentiment among the people these days. The young ones especially feel that they should have the right to choose their own careers," said Williams.

"Preposterous," said President Klens. "If we let them do that, then that would mean anyone could be part of the council. Or worse. They're just people. People who need to be controlled."

The door to her chamber opened as Officer Fernau and Seth Michaels walked in.

"You wished to see me," said Seth Michaels.

"Yes," replied President Klens. "What is going on here? You are in charge of maintaining order in the eastern region, and yet that wretch had the gall to challenge me. Challenge me! Do you not know what is going on here?"

"Madam president, I am all too aware."

"And the resistance. It grows each day. It has even spread to the western region. To my home!"

"It will be dealt with," said Seth Michaels.

"We can take care of her."

"No," said President Klens, "I don't wish to make her into a martyr."

"She won't be," replied Seth Michaels. "Officer Fernau has a better idea, and it may even result in the end of the resistance movement."

"I'm listening," said President Klens.

"She will lead us to the resistance. And when she does, we will eliminate them and her."

President Klens listened intently, liking what she heard. "Do it."

~ ~ ~

Dana hurried down the road toward Jesse's. As she passed George's small abode, a loud crash sounded from inside. Worried that something might have happened to him, Dana ran to the door and pushed it open.

"Where is it?" came George's voice. He stumbled around the room with an empty glass in his hand. His flailing movements told Dana he was intoxicated.

"George?" said Dana, tentatively.

George looked at her with half open eyes. "Well, hello there!"

"Are you all right?"

"Never better. Never better. Uh, perhaps you can help me find my whiskey."

Dana watched as her friend staggered around the room like an idiot. Worried, she stepped inside and closed the door. Her hand bumped something. Picking it up, Dana recognized it immediately as the jug of whiskey. She shook it. Empty.

"I think you drank it all," she said, putting the jug back down.

"Did I?" George looked at his glass and threw it over his shoulder. "Shit. Have to make more."

His feet tangled and he nearly fell to the floor. Dana rushed to him, and as she helped him to a chair, a concerned expression covered her face. She had never seen him like this. Actually, Dana never pegged George as one to drink.

"To my dear, dear wife." George raised his hand to a picture of a woman, holding it as though he actually held a glass. Sobbing filled the room as he leaned over the armrest of his chair and cried. Something plopped on the wood floor.

More concerned than ever, Dana picked it up and held it out to George. "George, what's wrong?"

He lifted his head. Seeing the locket in her outstretched hand, he took it, handling it with loving care. "This was my wife's."

Dana stared at the locket.

"She used to wear it all the time. Never kept any pictures in it. Just wore it cuz she thought it was pretty."

Dana listened intently. George had never opened up before, and she didn't like seeing him in this vulnerable state.

"She worked at the plant like me," continued George,

not able to stop now that he started. "One day, we were both scheduled to work in the incinerator."

A sinking feeling filled Dana's stomach. She guessed what had happened.

"Even in her grimy coveralls and bandanna, she was the prettiest thing I ever did see. We were separated by a few yards, you see. She was closest to the flames. I didn't think anything of it. Goes with the job, and she had been there many times before.

"Well, the flames got a bit out of control that day." George's voice cracked. He wiped his eyes and continued. "I looked over at her, and she looked right back at me knowing what was coming. I tried to reach her. I did! But, before I could, the floor fell out underneath her and she fell right in.

"I'll never forget her scream. I damn near threw myself in that day, but I just didn't have the courage."

Dana delicately placed her hand on George's to comfort him. She didn't know what to say. Nothing could take away the pain of losing someone close.

"That evening, I came back here. And on that table, there was this locket—her locket. She had forgotten to put it on that day. The one day she doesn't wear it and it's the day she died.

"That was today, you know. This very day."

The reason for George's drinking slapped Dana. *This was the anniversary of her death.* "George, I…" Dana broke off. What could she say?

George slumped over. Quickly, Dana caught him. She carefully helped him up and walked him over to his bed, covering him with a blanket. Dana picked up the locket and placed it on the table beside the bed.

"'That was brave what you did today," said George, "but you shouldn't have done it. They ain't likely to forget it."

"Let's worry about that later," said Dana. "You rest now."

"Sing to me, Lillian."

Dana started at the name before realizing that George's drunken mind was elsewhere. It was with his wife. Not wanting to disappoint him, she sang a melody that her mother once sang to her.

> Gone, but never far;
> invisible, but always near;
> bullied, but stronger than fear;
> trust Hope, your guiding star.

George's snores filled the room, telling Dana that he had fallen asleep. Not wanting to leave him alone like this, she settled in the chair. "To hell with the curfew," she whispered to herself.

CHAPTER TWELVE

Bits of merriment buzzed through the plant as those Dana's age hurried about, trying to spruce themselves up and prepare for their family reunion. True to her word, President Klens issued an order that those newly assigned to Waste Management be allowed to see their families. She even provided for their transportation.

A part of Dana wondered how long this good will would last. She shrugged it off as she pulled on her shirt. "Enjoy it for now," she told herself. She had her parents to greet.

"Which tie should I wear?" asked Sanders as he ran up to her, holding out two gaudy ties. Dana wondered where he got them.

"Why are you wearing a tie?" she asked.

"Because I haven't seen my mom for a long time and I want to look presentable."

"Hate to break it to you, Sanders, but ties do not go with our overalls," laughed Dana.

"Come on. Just pick one."

Dana gawked at him. Should she pick the black one with the pink polka dots or the yellow one with orange stripes? She covered her eyes and pointed. "That one."

Upon opening her eyes, Dana realized she had picked the yellow one with stripes. She hoped Sanders would approve.

"Good choice," he beamed as he ran off to put it on.

"Well," said Elsie, coming up from behind, "at least he won't look any more ridiculous than the rest of us."

Dana laughed. She finished tying her boots and ran off with Elsie to the meeting area. Excitement filled her.

"Oh, wait," said Dana, realizing she forgot her gift for her mom. "I'll meet up with you. I forgot something."

Dana ran back into the near empty barracks. She pulled out a wrapped box from underneath her bunk. As she jumped back to her feet, she ran into Mad Dog.

"Watch your back," he said.

Unsure of his motives, Dana took a step back.

"I mean it. Watch your back."

"Why are you telling me this?" Dana demanded.

"Because Tony was my brother. His mom took me in when mine died. What you did when the president was here—they don't like it.

Mad Dog walked away, leaving Dana alone. She fingered the smooth box, wondering what his message meant. Dana thought she had gotten away with it, since things had somewhat improved. But then she remembered the look on President Klens' face, that calculating look.

Realizing she wasted valuable time standing alone in the barracks, Dana rushed out. She pounded the metal stairs with her boots as she charged to the bottom level. Talking and commotion filled her ears when she entered the meeting area. Dana stopped in the doorway shocked by what she saw.

A feast fit for royalty filled the room. It had even been cleaned and decorated. A fountain rested on the table with clear, flowing water. Roast meat and fresh baked bread, along with trays of fresh vegetables, greeted her. It was as though the president had decided to break every rule of their society to have this. It had certainly quelled whatever Dana had almost ignited.

"Dana!" Elsie ran up to her. "Here she is, mom, dad."

Dana watched as Elsie walked up with her parents.

"Dana, these are my parents. And this is Dana."

"Pleased to meet you," said Elsie's mother. "Elsie has told us so much about you."

"Thank you," said Dana.

"Where are your folks?" asked Elsie's dad.

"I'm still looking for them," said Dana.

"Oh, well, don't let us keep you," said Elsie's mother.

Dana wished them well and parted. She wandered the area. As she strolled by the table of food, she snatched pieces of roast beef and bread.

"Dana!"

Dana whirled around. Her mother waved to her, holding her father's hand. Together, they ran up to her, enveloping her in a giant hug.

"Oh, we've missed you," said her mother. "My poor girl. You never should have been sent here."

"It's okay, mom," said Dana. "Here. I got you both something."

Her mother took the small box and opened it, revealing the coins inside. They were what was left over from the sale of Kenny's watch.

"Dana, you shouldn't have," said her mother.

Her father quickly took the box and shoved it in his deep pocket. "Where did you get it?"

"Don't worry about it," said Dana. "I know about the underground markets, and I know you do too. I want you to have it."

"No, you should keep it," said her mother.

"Mom, please," said Dana.

"Why the urgency?" asked her father.

"Because I have a feeling that things are about to get worse," said Dana.

"What makes you say that?" asked her mother.

"Because when the president came here..."

"Yes, we heard about that," said her father. "All of Dystopia did."

"Really?" said Dana, intrigued.

"Word like that spreads fast," replied her father. "But be careful. Your temper will get you into trouble one day."

"Oh, that's enough of that," said her mother. "If you keep a low profile, Dana, I'm sure this will all blow over. But for now, let us just enjoy this moment."

Dana hugged her parents again.

The rest of the time, Dana spent with her parents and friends gabbing and eating. Not knowing when the dream would end, she wanted to enjoy as much of it as she could. The hours soon passed and the buzzer sounded.

Dana noticed Jesse concealed in the shadows. She

motioned for Jesse to leave, hoping the girl would head back home. Before the caterers had a chance to run off with the display of food, she stuffed a cloth napkin with it. Dana shoved it under her shirt, thankful that it was baggy enough to hide it.

She ran back to her parents before they boarded the bus. "Good-bye, sweetheart," said her mother, planting a kiss on her forehead.

"Bye, mom." Dana hugged her mom again.

"Take care of yourself," said her father as he embraced her.

Waving to her parents, Dana's heart ached terribly as she immediately missed them. She didn't know when she would see them again.

Before the officers could send her back to the barracks with the rest, Dana darted away. She had a friend to visit. She snuck to the main ventilation shaft. George had shown her the way.

Glancing about her, Dana opened the grate and lifted herself inside. Carefully, she close it. Moving slowly, she crawled on her hands and knees through the ducting, taking care not to squish the food she carried. Her knee caused the metal to bend slightly, releasing a popping sound. Cursing, Dana listened for signs that someone had heard. Nothing.

Carefully, she crept through the ventilation until she came to another opening. Peeking through the slits, Dana saw that no officers were around. She popped the latch and opened the door. Lowering herself to the ground, Dana quickly shut the door and ran off. Since the ventilation shaft took her past the fence, she had only to make it to Shackville before anyone in the towers noticed her. Breathing hard, Dana ran as fast as she could until she reached cover.

The little village of those who lived in Waste Management had not changed. A few sat in rocking chairs smoking, while others hung up their laundry after washing it in giant buckets. Dana sped through their streets and to Jesse's home. She knocked twice before letting herself in.

"Dana," said Nana. She sat in her chair with a pair of knitting needles.

Jesse jumped to her feet and wrapped her tiny arms around Dana's waist.

"I brought you something." She unfolded the cloth with the food.

"Dana, you shouldn't have," said Nana.

"It's okay. They won't miss it. It was part of…"

"Yes, I heard about the feast going on up there," said Nana. "That is certainly the first time it has ever happened."

"And probably the last," muttered Dana. "Take it."

Nana took the food and placed it in her kitchen. "We certainly thank you."

Jesse yanked on Dana's arm. "I got something to show you."

Dana allowed herself to be led outside as Jesse guided her. She took her to a small pit of sand with what looked like a metal pole sticking out of the ground.

"Watch," said Jesse.

Jesse walked up to the pole and jumped on it. Clinging to it, she used her legs to push herself upward as she held on. Slowly, the girl reached the top. Once there, she released her grip and slid back to the bottom.

"Did you see? Did you see? I can climb to the top and no one else can."

"That's was wonderful," praised Dana.

"I bet you can't do it," said Jesse.

"You're probably right," said Dana.

"Try it," Jesse demanded.

Knowing she wasn't going to get out of a challenge made by a seven-year-old, Dana approached the pole. She grasped the cold steel with her hands and jumped on it. Wrapping her legs around it, she pushed herself upward. Her strong muscles pulled her up easily. Halfway to the top, Dana decided to not disappoint Jesse. She released her grip and fell to the bottom, landing on her rear with a thud.

"I told you you couldn't do it," laughed Jesse.

"You sure did," said Dana.

"You're not as strong as me."

"Nope. But I will be someday."

Dana reached for the girl and tickled her tummy. Squeals of delight rang out into the night as Jesse laughed. Realizing that the sun dipped dangerously low, Dana decided it was time to leave.

"We should go."

She walked Jesse back to the hut, braiding the girl's hair as they walked. Jesse kept picking up what flowers there were and handed them to Dana. Chuckling, she put them in Jesse's hair.

"There," said Dana, "now you look like a princess."

"Will you come visit again?" asked Jesse.

Dana looked down upon the girl and her red hair. "Of course I will."

Overjoyed at having a friend, Jesse hugged Dana again and went inside.

Dana headed back. She twirled one of the flowers Jesse had given her in her hand, smiling to herself. Her heart felt light and happy. *Why can't everyday be like this?* Skipping down the street, Dana never noticed the officers watching her.

Suddenly, arms seized her, jerking her off her feet. Before she could scream, a gag was shoved in her mouth, choking her. She kicked and flung her arms everywhere. A fist punched her. Despite the pain, Dana continued to struggle. Finally, a bag slipped over her head, and her feet left the ground as her attackers carted her away.

Eyes watched the entire incident from the windows of their homes. No one helped; they were frozen by fear.

CHAPTER THIRTEEN

Dana's already bruised bottom stung even more as men dumped her in a chair. Someone ripped the bag off her head and the gag from her mouth. Her eyes hurt from the bright light that shone in them. Blinking, she waited for them to adjust.

The plastic tie cut deep into her flesh as she attempted to free her wrists. She felt warm blood ooze down her skin as each of her movements made the tie tighter. The throbbing bruise on her face distracted her.

"Dana Ginary," said a cold voice.

The man it belonged to paced the room. Only his boots were revealed in the light.

"Who are you?" demanded Dana. "What am I doing here?"

"You should already know the answer to that."

Dana guessed why. President Klens was getting even. She scolded herself for being so stupid.

"Now, you had your little outburst. The president allowed you to see your family. All is well."

"Then why am I here?" Dana demanded again.

Colonel Fernau stared at Dana. "I think I will let the First Councilman explain that."

He knocked on the door. Immediately, it opened, and in stepped Seth Michaels in a crisp, pressed suit. Kenny followed behind his father.

Dana watched them through the strands of her hair that remained plastered to her face.

"Dana Ginary," said Seth Michaels. "My son has told me a lot about you. I expected to meet someone of better repute."

Dana remained silent. She had no idea where this was going.

"I am willing to sum up your latest outbursts against the state as the mere whim of youth. But I want something in return." A foreboding tension filled his voice.

"And what would that be?" asked Dana, keeping her voice under control as she struggled against the plastic tie around her wrists.

"Surely we don't need this, Colonel," said Seth Michaels.

Colonel Fernau stepped over to Dana and cut the tie loose.

Relieved, Dana rubbed her sore wrists; blood trickled down her fingers. Her eyes darted from one man to the next, unsure of what they wanted.

"As you are aware, the resistance movement has been growing these past several months. President Klens would like to see them eliminated. I am sure you are aware of the lies they spread."

"I wouldn't know," said Dana. "I haven't met anyone from the resistance."

"Haven't you?" Seth Michaels arched an eyebrow at her. "I hear that you are friendly with a man named George Saule."

"He's no…" began Dana.

"I'm afraid he is. Though perhaps he did not wish you to know."

Dana started to realize what this was about.

Seth Michaels continued. "I am offering you a chance to be forgiven for your past transgressions. We know you have been to the underground market and that you went with George. Don't bother asking how. We know everything."

Dana glanced at her forearm. She knew she had been implanted with a chip since birth, but it never occurred to her that it could be a tracking device. But if it was, then why couldn't…

"You can't track them, can you?"

The looks on the others' faces told Dana she had guessed right. The members of the resistance had found a way to keep from being tracked with the chips in their arms.

"I knew we would understand each other," purred Seth Michaels. "No, we cannot track them. They have found a way to keep our devices from picking up their chips. They have a mechanism that bounces the signal everywhere so that we cannot pinpoint it.

"But if we had someone on the inside, that person could tell us when and where they meet."

"I am not part of the resistance," said Dana.

"No, but you can get yourself in."

"How?"

"We will stage something. A little show that will make them think they can trust you."

Dana didn't like this. "You want me to betray them. To gain their trust and then turn on them. I won't do it."

"Miss Ginary, I suggest you reconsider the matter," said Seth Michaels.

"Do you miss your parents?" said Colonel Fernau. "It would be unfortunate if they never returned home."

Panic filled Dana. She had last seen her parents get on the bus headed north to the district where they lived. "What are you saying?"

"Unfortunately, they were found in possession of contraband items. The penalty is most severe," said Colonel Fernau. "And then there are your friends, Elsie and the other one, Sanders. It would be unfortunate if they suffered an accident."

Pure hatred filled Dana's eyes as she stared at the colonel.

"Or perhaps, you only care for that red-headed girl. Jesse, is that her name? I hear her grandmother is very ill despite the medicine you managed to procure for her."

"You son of a..." began Dana.

"The point is," said Seth Michaels, "we can make all of this go away if you do as we ask. We will even wipe out all of the red flags on your record."

"By blackmailing me?"

"I call it persuasion," said Colonel Fernau.

"Think about it," said Seth Michaels. "This could be your one chance to get out of Waste Management.

"If you succeed, I will personally see to it that you get the most comfortable job in this region. You and your parents will be allowed to move out of the province they live in and into more luxurious accommodations. You need never fear hunger or poverty."

Dana said nothing.

"You don't know these people," said Seth Michaels, "and you do not owe them anything."

Dana continued to remain silent, her mind racing over her prospects.

"I can make all of your problems go away."

Gradually, Dana looked up at Kenny's father. Her eyes darted over to Kenny, who stood silently in a corner of the room. "And you called yourself my friend."

Kenny whispered something to his father. Immediately, Seth Michaels motioned for Colonel Fernau to follow him as he left the interrogation room.

Kenny unplugged the surveillance camera and locked the door. "I am your friend, Dana."

"And I accepted your gift."

"I gave you that watch because I knew you needed it."

Dana looked at the floor.

"Dana, please. They are only offering you this chance because I begged my father to. President Klens wanted you killed. But I convinced my father to give you this chance to redeem yourself."

"Redeem myself? I'm not the one using fear to control people."

"Oh, forget the politics, Dana. This is beyond that. Our system works as long as everyone follows the law. If you weren't so stubborn, we wouldn't be here right now."

"Not everyone can be as pliable as you," spat Dana.

"Oh, cut the crap! What is the resistance to you, except a bunch of people who want to start trouble? We all have our place in society. We can't just go around always thinking about what we want."

"But isn't that what you do? Isn't that what President Klens does?"

"Huh?"

"You still believe in this system don't you, Kenny? Even after everything you have just witnessed."

"Everyone benefits," said Kenny.

"Really? Am I benefiting right now?" Dana eyed the person she had thought was her friend. "Ask a question. Any question. Challenge the system in some way and you will find yourself exactly where I am."

"But I am offering you this chance to change all that," said Kenny.

"And I called you my friend."

"I am your friend! I don't want to see you here. I didn't know Colonel Fernau was going to arrest your parents. That was his idea. Do what they want. Give them the resistance and you will go free."

"Do you really believe that?" asked Dana.

"Can you afford not to?"

Dana and Kenny locked eyes. She saw in his eyes that he believed what he said, even though she did not. Still, her parents' lives were at stake.

"Do it for yourself. Do it for your parents."

"Where are they?" asked Dana.

"In a containment facility. Don't worry. I'll see to it that they are comfortable. My father assured me that they will be kept safe as long as you do as he asks. When you are finished, you will all go home."

Tears welled up in Dana's eyes. She choked them back, not wanting to give them the satisfaction of making her cry. *What choice do I have?*

"Promise me, Kenny. Promise me that nothing will happen to my parents."

"I promise."

"Then, I'll do it."

Relieved, Kenny opened the door and let his father and the colonel back in. "She has agreed."

"Excellent," said Seth Michaels.

"You will stick close to George Saule," said Colonel Fernau. "Very close. We believe that sometime within the next week, he will meet up with the resistance again. When he does, follow him."

"But how will I gain their trust?" asked Dana.

"We will take care of that," said Colonel Fernau. "The next time he goes into the city, make sure you are with him. I don't care how you do it.

"Once there, some of my men will attack you both. Don't worry. They'll have orders to not kill either of you, and they will know to let you win. But make the fight look real. You may end up with a bruise or two."

"It is acceptable," said Dana, her voice hollow.

"After that, it will be up to you to convince the other members," said Colonel Fernau. "You will identify the leaders. We will take care of the rest."

"We are all counting on you," said Seth Michaels.

"I understand," said Dana.

"Very well," replied Seth Michaels. "Take Dana back to Waste Management. If anyone asks where you have been, tell them you were visiting that girl."

"Yes, sir."

Dana allowed herself to be hauled out of the chair and led away. Her will to fight had deserted her.

"You did well, my boy," said Seth Michaels to his son. "Positively well."

"Thank you, father. What will happen to her parents?"

"They will be transferred to a more secure location," replied Seth Michaels.

"More secure?" said Kenny.

"Do not worry," Colonel Fernau stepped in. "I am having them taken to a place where they will be comfortable. It is more of a penthouse. They will be under guard, but they will have every comfort life can offer. It is for their security as well as ours."

"Oh," said Kenny. "I did promise her."

"You will keep your promise just like I always keep mine." Seth Michaels wrapped an arm around his son. "Now, it is time we return home. There is much to do."

CHAPTER  FOURTEEN

The squelching and whistling of the conveyer belt as Dana worked beside it rattled her nerves. Thoughts of the previous night plagued her mind. How was she to betray her friends and save her parents? After hours of wrestling with her conscience, Dana realized that in this society, one was not allowed to have friends.

She picked up a plastic container that once held some kind of liquid. Carelessly, Dana tossed it on the conveyer belt that went straight into the recycling portion of the plant. It landed with a thump. Despite being tired, she raked at the pile of refuse she stood upon, sifting through it for more recyclable items. She picked up a half-broken glass bottle and tossed it into the chute for glass items.

"Hey," said Elsie as she and Sanders walked up.

"What are you two doing here?" asked Dana. "I thought you were working in the metals area."

"We bribed the officer to let us come here," replied Elsie.

"Oh."

"What happened to you yesterday?" asked Sanders.

"I'm not sure what you mean," said Dana, avoiding the question.

"Yes you do," said Elise.

Dana looked over at an officer watching her every move. She didn't know how many people knew of the arrangement between her and Seth Michaels, but she didn't want to take any chances. "I can't talk about it."

"What's wrong, Dana," said Elsie. "You seem different."

"Maybe because I am," said Dana.

"Why won't you tell us what happened?" said Sanders.

"Because... I went to Jesse's last night like I usually do. I forgot about the time and had to sneak in. I was lucky I didn't get caught."

Officer Burroughs strolled past. He looked in Dana's direction, and she knew that he wanted to know the contents of her conversation with Elsie and Sanders.

"It might be best if you two aren't seen with me quite so much," said Dana, walking off.

Sanders and Elsie watched her go.

"Lost track of time," said Sanders. "Dana never loses track of time."

"Yeah," mused Elsie. "Something else is going on here. Let's get back to work."

Dana glanced up as her two friends disappeared. She hated lying to them.

"Dana Ginary," said an officer. "You are wanted in Officer Burroughs' office."

Dana dropped her rake and followed the uniformed man to Officer Burroughs' office. They hiked up a metal staircase that curved in circles. The higher they went, the more anxious Dana became. She wiped her sweaty palms on her pants.

"In." The officer held the door open.

Nerves going haywire, Dana entered the small office. She immediately noticed the big window that overlooked the plant. It was one of those two-way mirrors.

"Miss Ginary," said Officer Burroughs, indicating for her to take a seat.

Dana obliged.

"I noticed that you were talking with your two friends."

"I always talk with them," said Dana, her heart pounding so hard she thought it would force its way out of her chest.

"I want to know what you were discussing."

"Nothing special."

"Miss Ginary, I am aware of your arrangement with the First Councilman. Colonel Fernau has told me what I need to know."

Not everything, thought Dana.

"So I am asking you once more. What did you tell them?"

"Nothing," said Dana. "They just wanted to know why I was back so late. I told them I had visited another friend and lost track of time."

The thoughtful look on Officer Burroughs' face told her that he only half-believed her. "In the future, you might want to spend less time with them and more with George Saule, gaining his trust."

"Won't that look suspicious?" asked Dana.

"Pardon?"

Dana fiddled with her hands before finally placing them in her lap. Her pulse thudded so hard that she wondered if everyone else heard it as well. "If I change my habits, don't you think that would look suspicious even to them?"

"That is excellent thinking," said Officer Burroughs.

Dana released the breath she had been holding.

"However, my officers and I will be watching your every move," said Officer Burroughs. "If you sneeze, we will know about it."

He waved an officer over. "In fact, we have decided that you should wear this."

Officer Burroughs held up a shirt.

"This top button has a camera built into it. It will record everything you say and do. Put it on." Officer Burroughs tossed the shirt to Dana.

She clumsily caught it. Realizing that no one was going to give her an ounce of privacy, Dana stood up and unbuttoned her shirt. As quickly as she could, she put the other one on.

"Make certain that you do not take it off," said Officer Burroughs.

He motioned for her to leave. Immediately, an officer wrapped his gloved hand around her arm and pushed her toward the door.

"And remember, we will be watching everything you do."

Dana's heart sank. If she thought she was a prisoner before, she was even more of one now.

Once freed from Officer Burroughs' office, Dana ran to a posted schedule to see where she would be spending her afternoon. Her name had been placed next to George's for the incinerator. *Big surprise*. Before she could be yelled at, Dana rushed off to the bottom level where the incinerator awaited her.

Once there, she quickly put on the gloves that ran up the length of her arm and grabbed a rake. The roar of the incinerator pounded her ears, giving her a headache. The thought of jumping in floated through her mind. Dana pushed it away. *How will that help my parents?*

"Well, you look a little worse for the wear," greeted George as she took her place next to him. He flung a bunch of garbage into the fires.

"What?" said Dana.

"There's bags under your eyes," said George. "Didn't get much sleep last night, did ya?"

"Uh, no," said Dana. "I was a bit preoccupied."

"By what?"

"You know, all that excitement of being able to see my parents."

A lump formed in Dana's throat at the mention of her parents. She immediately swallowed it back before she could betray anything.

"George," said Dana, "I need to get to the market again."

George stepped closer so they wouldn't have to shout. "What for?"

"Things I need and can't get here. Look, it's personal stuff. I still have a few coins left over."

"Not tonight, dearie," said George.

"Why?"

George gave her a questioning look.

"When then?"

"Tomorrow soon enough?"

"Yeah. Can I bring Elsie and Sanders?"

"What for?"

Dana's mind raced as she tried to figure out a reason. She didn't even know why she asked.

"Sanders is good at math. He'd be able to tell me right off if I'm being cheated."

That line of reasoning made sense to George. "And Elsie?"

"No reason," mumbled Dana.

"Yeah, sure. They seem honest enough. Considering the amount of officers that go there, what's a couple more wayward souls?"

The last comment stung Dana. He spoke of honesty, and she was trying to get him to reveal his secrets for her own gain. "Tomorrow night then."

Dana scooped a pile of refuse into the flames. Her eyes flickered to the camera on her shirt. Emptiness filled her.

CHAPTER FIFTEEN

The next evening came all too quickly. Taking deep breaths, Dana calmed her nerves. She had a feeling that the resistance met in or around the underground market. The bit of code George used the last time tipped her off.

"Ready?" whispered Dana to Elsie.

Elsie and Sanders had readily agreed to come with her when she asked. They had each put on dark clothing to avoid detection while sneaking around at night.

Dana led them to the hole in the barracks. Not wanting everything they did recorded, she feigned being cold and zipped her jacket all the way up as though it was a force of habit.

They squeezed through the hole and into the chilly night air. The temperature had dropped. Dana knew that summer had gone and winter was coming.

"Hurry," urged Dana.

They ran through the plant, their boots making soft thumps on the semi-frozen ground. Sticking to the concealed areas, the three hurried to the fence where the wires were loose.

"Be careful," whispered Dana. "These spikes are sharp."

She held the barbed wire up for Elsie and Sanders. Sanders' pants caught on one of the spikes. Quickly, Dana ripped him free, a soft tearing sound filling her ears. Making certain the guard towers looked the other way, she slipped through the fence.

"Hurry."

Dana pushed them down the hill and past the trees and bushes that provided cover. She had no idea how many of Officer Burroughs' men knew about her arrangement, but she didn't want to be caught outside after curfew. Though she might be spared, Elsie and Sanders would not be so lucky.

They jogged through Shackville and to George's small shack. Dana rapped on the door. It opened and George stepped out. He waved them onward and they all ran out of the area.

George led them to the train area and the cart that he and Dana had used before. Stealthily, they moved through the darkness. The gravel beneath their feet crunched with each movement. With great care, they hopped over the raised tracks so as not to trip.

"On," said George when they reached the cart.

Dana took one end of the handle and George the other. Together, they moved as one, pushing the rail cart down the tracks and toward the city.

Squeak. Squeak.

Dana winced each time the wheels squeaked. She hoped it wouldn't attract attention. They rode it to the city limits before coming to a halt.

Quickly, they disembarked and ran through a hole in the city wall. George urged them to hurry up. Once through, they quickly darted down an alley, turning many corners before George halted them.

Peeking around a corner, he looked up and down the street. Dana began to recognize the area some, but even she was a bit confused about where they were.

"Come on," said George.

They dashed across the street and down another alley. Now Dana definitely knew where they were. She recognized the rotted door that George opened for them.

"In."

Loud plops echoed around them as they trotted down the hollow, wooden steps to the door. George knocked on it like he did the last time and repeated the passphrase.

"Back again, eh?" said the man as he opened the door. "Folk can never get enough of this place."

Dana just smiled in response.

"Right then," said George. "I imagine you folk got everything handled from here. I got some things to do, so you all do your shopping and meet back here in an hour."

"Thanks, George," said Dana. She wanted to know where he went, but knew she had to maintain the fiction she had given him.

"Let's go," said Elsie, grabbing Dana's arm and leading her into the throng of vendors and shops. People bustled about with their treasures, visiting stall after stall.

"Leather cases!" shouted one man. "Genuine leather!"

"What would I want with a leather case?" mumbled Sanders.

"Maybe it could hold that big head of yours," teased Elsie. Dana chuckled.

"So, what did you need from here?" asked Elsie.

"What?"

Dana kicked herself. She hadn't even thought about what she was supposed to have needed from this place. Dana glanced around at the various vendors and their wares. She spotted bags, food items, knick knacks, and clothing items.

A scarf rack caught her attention. "This," said Dana trotting over to it. She snatched a purple scarf with silver trimming.

"A scarf?" asked Elsie.

"Yeah," said Dana. "It's getting cold outside, and you know the barracks aren't heated."

Elsie reconsidered the matter. She picked out a bright red one and tried it on. Admiring herself in the mirror, Elsie pranced around, pretending to be a lady of influence.

Sanders watched her as though she had lost her mind.

"How much?" Dana asked the saleslady.

"Two coins."

Dana handed over the money, and she and Elsie walked away with their purchases.

"Was that all you wanted?" asked Sanders.

"Yeah, but we can wander around," replied Dana.

"Might as well," said Elsie.

Dana showed them around. They stopped at a man that sold apples, and each purchased one. As they sat to the side munching, Sanders and Elsie gabbed about something near their home. Dana spotted George. She leaned over a bit trying to see where he went. Two men she had never seen before greeted him. After greeting one another, they walked up some stairs and through a door.

"Dana?"

Dana whipped around. Elsie and Sanders both stared at her with concern.

"What's wrong?" asked Elsie.

"Nothing," said Dana, a bit too quickly. "Just lost in my thoughts."

"Oh," Elsie's tone revealed she didn't believe her.

"Well, I want to check out that guy with all of those gadgets," said Sanders. He rambled on about how exciting it would be to have them, using so many technical terms that Dana tuned him out.

"Alright, geek boy," said Elsie, "you go have fun with your toys while Dana and I go do more shopping."

They parted. Time passed quickly as Elsie and Dana went from one shop to another. They looked at various bags and even jewelry.

Dana picked up a clunky necklace.

"No, hun," Elsie shook her head. "That is not for you." She picked up a pair of earrings. "These would work better."

Carefully, Dana took them. She held them up, admiring them. Elsie knew her fashion. Dana bought the earrings, while Elsie made off with the necklace she had originally considered buying.

"Fresh milk! Oh, hey there," said the man who sold milk.

Dana stopped. She had forgotten all about him. The cow still stood in its pen, chewing on hay and ignoring everything.

"Brought a friend with you?" said the milk salesman.

"Yeah," said Dana.

"Well, just got this this morning."

"Two bottles," said Dana handing over the coins. She gave a bottle to Elsie, who looked at it skeptically. "Go on, drink it," said Dana, popping the cork off hers.

Wrinkling her nose, Elsie sniffed the milk and took a sip. She smacked her lips as a satisfied grin crossed her face. "That ain't bad."

"Told you," said Dana.

"Here," said the man. "These are on the house." He gave them two more bottles.

"Thanks," said Elsie.

"Let's find Sanders," said Dana. "Our hour is almost up."

After worming their way through the crowds of people, they finally found Sanders in a heated argument over the price of some item.

"I'm telling you, it isn't worth more than 15," said Sanders.

"And I says the price is 25," replied the man behind the counter.

"Twenty-five! That's thievery."

"If ya don't like it, then go elsewhere."

"There isn't anywhere else to go."

"Then pay up or leave," said the man.

"I will not," barked Sanders. "What if I start telling people that you fix these so that they are forced to buy new parts from you?"

"Why I never—you wouldn't."

Sanders put his item down and started to walk away.

"Wait! Perhaps, I could negotiate."

"Fifteen," said Sanders.

"Fifteen then."

Sanders handed over the coins.

"There now, get out of here. And don't come back!"

"What was that all about?" demanded Elsie.

"Just haggling," said Sanders. "I only had the 15 coins."

"Come on, let's go." Elsie pulled Sanders along, and they all headed for the exit where George waited for them.

Once again, Dana noticed the same two men shaking hands with him as they parted. "Who were they?" she asked, trying to sound innocent.

"Just a couple of friends," replied George. "You all ready to leave?"

"Yeah," said Sanders.

The man at the door opened it for them. "Ya'll come back now," he said to them.

The door shut behind them, bolting into place. Once again, Dana was left on the stairs with more questions than answers and an empty feeling in her stomach.

CHAPTER SIXTEEN

A week had passed and Dana was no nearer to getting George to take her to the resistance movement. She had no idea how to do it. Frustrated, she slammed her locker shut.

Colonel Fernau stood right behind her. "Stressed?"

Instinctively, Dana jumped back. His malicious demeanor frightened her. *This is a man who wouldn't hesitate to kill his mother.*

"What makes you say that?" Dana tried to sound casual, but her shaky voice betrayed her.

"It has been a week, and we have heard little about your progress," said Colonel Fernau.

"There hasn't been much."

"Perhaps you do not understand the gravity of your situation."

"I understand it fine," said Dana. "It's just George does not fully trust me. The resistance is a tight-knit group. They aren't about to let me in without reason to."

"Yes, well we'll just remedy that." Colonel Fernau used his stick to turn Dana's head toward a window. "You see those people out there? Dregs of society. They are the ones who did not understand how things work. So they are here; where their lack of understanding will not harm anyone. You are quickly becoming one of them."

Colonel Fernau's dangerous undertone unnerved Dana.

"The little problem of yours will soon be at an end."

Dana eyed the man, wondering what he referred to.

"It has been arranged," continued Colonel Fernau, "Just make certain that you are in that mass of rubble known as Shackville. When you see George head out, follow him. The resistance is meeting tonight."

"How do you…"

"Oh, I forgot that you would be completely unaware of such things. We decided to do something that would push them to have a meeting. This is your chance to find out where they are. The little show we mentioned earlier will happen then. Just make certain that you are near George tonight when it happens."

"But…"

"Don't screw it up," warned Colonel Fernau, his face close to Dana's so she smelled the bourbon on his breath.

"Yes, sir."

Colonel Fernau left the locker room. "This will be your one and only chance. Once in, it is up to you to gain their trust. Your parents' lives depend on it."

The colonel left. Dana stared after him. She leaned against a locker, the cold metal reminding her of her dire situation.

As was agreed, Dana snuck out of the plant and down to

Shackville immediately after supper. Smoke spilled from the smoke stacks behind her. No guards patrolled the area she moved in. Undoubtedly, she thought, that was all arranged for my benefit. Dana didn't care. She had one thought on her mind, to wait for George to leave his hut and follow him.

The sun settled low on the horizon, setting earlier and earlier each day. Dana found a spot where she could easily see George's front door and not be noticed. She rubbed her cold hands together; her fingers had gone stiff. Blowing on them, Dana wished George would hurry up.

A creak grabbed her attention. George had opened his door. He poked his head out, glanced around, then slipped out and ran off down the hill. Dana jumped to her feet. Pins and needles filled her cramped legs as the circulation returned. Ignoring her stiffness, she took off after the man.

Dana hugged buildings as she followed George. *Please don't spot me.* George continued unaware of her presence. Dana dashed down the hill after him, crouching behind bushes when she reached the bottom. George whirled around and surveyed the area behind him. Staying extreme-ly still, Dana watched. When George continued on, Dana bolted from her spot.

Surprised, Dana paused a moment when she noticed that George did not go to the cart he had used to get to the city with her. Instead, he took the bus.

"Why is he taking the bus?" Dana whispered.

She knew it was not illegal to take the bus, and one could ride it freely until the midnight curfew.

Dana dashed after George. She had no idea how she would follow him on the bus without being noticed. She stopped behind a pole when she neared the bus stop. The roar of a diesel engine told her the bus approached. It stopped and George hopped on.

Stamping her feet, Dana panicked. How was she to follow him? She spotted an abandoned moped. A deliveryman had just gotten off it. Quickly, Dana ran to it, hopped on, and took off after the bus.

"Hey!" yelled the man it belonged to.

Thankful that Kenny had allowed her to use his moped when they were kids, she hunkered low for the least resistance and put it at top speed. The bus pulled to a halt and picked up more passengers. Dana slowed. She watched as the new people boarded the bus and pulled away again. Turning in its direction, Dana sped after it. She hoped she wouldn't miss seeing George get off.

The spurting engine backfired a bit as Dana pushed the moped hard. It hasn't been well-maintained, she thought to herself. Didn't matter. She had a job to do.

The bus stopped again. Dana pulled in behind a car and waited. An exchange took place as people got off and others stepped on. The squeaking of the doors told her the bus was moving once again.

She put the moped in gear and charged after the bus. No one paid attention to her. They all assumed she worked for the Delivery Service Department. Her eyes watered from the cold air that whipped around her.

The bus stopped for a fourth time. George got off. Quickly, Dana plowed through the streets to catch up to George. When she reached the bus stop, she came to a screeching halt. Dana jumped off the moped, allowing it to crash into a row of bikes. She leapt behind a giant planter just as George turned around to see what the commotion was. He shrugged his shoulders and continued.

Dana jumped to her feet. Following at a distance, she stuck to the shadows. George continued on, unconcerned that someone might be following him. He stopped. Dana hugged the outside wall of a brick building.

Two men approached George. *This must be it.* Dana watched as the men pushed George around and he tried to walk away. Soon they came to blows.

George took a fist to the mouth. He returned the favor. A grunt sounded as George took a hit to the stomach. Having waited long enough, Dana plowed into one of the attackers and knocked him to the ground. His partner socked her in the face. The sting of the impact dazed her.

Dana had been warned that they would make it look real. She felt that they were only told not to kill her. Blocking an attack, Dana rammed her fist into one of the attacker's nose. She elbowed him again in the stomach. The one she had knocked down charged. Instantly, George stepped in, catching the man's fist, and threw him into a pile of empty crates.

"Let's get out of here," yelled one of the attackers. He grabbed his partner and the two darted away.

"Thanks," said George.

"Anytime," replied Dana, wiping blood from the corner of her lip.

"What are you doing here?" asked George.

"What are you?" replied Dana. "Why'd they attack you?"

"Muggers most like," said George. "They don't need a reason."

Dana said nothing.

"Really, Dana," George's tone grew serious, "why are you here?"

Dana thought quickly. She needed a story, and once again, she wished she had thought of one beforehand. "I needed to be in the city for reasons that are my own."

"Fair enough."

"What about you?"

"Same."

"You going to be all right?" asked Dana, not sure how to steer this to her accompanying George to wherever he was headed.

"Yeah, I'll be fine. This isn't my first skirmish."

"Then I guess we'll…"

Officers patrolled by. George seized Dana's hand and pulled her along. They hid behind a dumpster. Slowly, the officers moved past them, but their shadows still draped across the walk.

"Come on," said George. "You might as well come with me. No use you getting arrested."

Dana didn't respond.

"You are not to tell anyone about where you've been, understand?"

"Yes," said Dana.

"I mean it."

"I understand," Dana reiterated.

George took her wrist and dragged her down the alley. They turned a corner and another. Pausing, George looked behind them. No one followed. He steered Dana through the maze of back alleys until coming upon a door.

Dana instantly noted that this door was different from the one that led to the underground market. George knocked twice and opened the door, pulling Dana inside. He shut it silently.

Dana stopped short the moment George let go of her. Men and women stood gathered around a table, staring at her and looking none too friendly. She desperately hoped that she could convince them she was their friend.

"George?" said a man with dark skin and a mustache.

"I wasn't followed," said George.

"Who's she?" demanded the same man.

"A friend," said George.

"A friend?"

"My name is Dana…"

"I wasn't talking to you," snapped the man.

"Hey," said George, "you calm down. She works at the plant with me. I was attacked in the streets by two hoodlums and she came to my rescue."

"How convenient," sneered the man.

Dana didn't like him.

"What were you doing in the city?" the man asked her.

"None of your business," replied Dana.

"I'll make it my business."

"Will you calm down?" said another to the man that had been hostile towards Dana. "Charles here is not very trusting."

No kidding, thought Dana.

"My name is Simon Reeds," said the kinder man. He pushed his glasses up his face. "This here is Charles Wayneberg."

"I still want to know why she happened to be where he was when he was attacked," said Charles.

"She was probably in the city for the same reason that many sneak into the city," said Simon. "Let it rest."

"What if she's a plant?"

"Oh, now see here," said George.

"Charles," Simon's calm voice commanded attention, "the resistance is bigger than all of us. And besides, I don't think she would ever intentionally harm us."

Dana watched the proceedings, trying to figure out who was in charge.

"Let her stay," said a woman, whom Dana learned was Amy Nelson. Her muscled arms made Dana wish she never got in a fistfight with her. "You can take a seat over there."

George approached the table, while Dana scooted to the far side of the room. Positioning herself in the corner, she just watched and listened. *What have I gotten myself into?*

"As you all know," said Simon, "the government has been trying to infiltrate us for some time."

Charles glared at Dana at that statement.

"I am almost certain that they will succeed at some point," continued Simon.

"What makes you say that?" asked another in the room.

"It is only a matter of time. Our business is dangerous. That is why I said that our movement must be bigger than just those of us in this room. Now, they have branded us as traitors, terrorists, and extremists. What we need to do is get our message out."

"What?"

Simon spoke again. "Most people know that there is something terribly wrong about our society. They know that the government controls every aspect of their lives. Some don't care. But most want things to change. They just don't know how. What we need to do is remind them of a time when none of this existed. We need to remind them that people were meant to live free.

"Now our methods should be peaceful."

"You do realize that we won't be able to achieve our ends without a fight," said Charles.

"I realize that," said Simon, "but we should try peaceful means first. War should always be a last resort."

"It won't work," muttered Charles.

"Always the hothead," said Amy.

"Enough, you two," said Simon. "Look, I have no doubt that our fight won't be won without a few bullets, but for now, let's try changing people's hearts. Until they decide that they want to live free, what does it matter if we go down guns blazing?"

"So what do you want to do?" asked Amy.

"The government controls the media," said Simon. "Every night at around six, the news is on, and most people watch it because they have little choice. I propose that we air a video with our message at that time."

"What?" said Charles. "And how do you propose we do this? Just walk in?"

"That's a good idea," said Dana.

Everyone turned to her.

"At the plant, discarded uniforms of the media center are usually stored for a while before being incinerated. George and I could lift a few of them for us to wear to get inside."

"That is an idea," said George, "and she's right about the uniforms."

"I have procured the passes," said Amy.

"Good," said Simon.

"We need a timetable," said Charles.

"We'll discuss that later," said Simon. "I have the tape already made with what we want to say. But there is the question of breaking the access codes at the media center."

"Leave that to me," said Dana.

"What?" said George.

"I can get us past the access codes," said Dana.

"How?" challenged Charles.

Dana thought a moment. She had seen an opportunity to prove useful and gain the trust of these people, but she did not want Colonel Fernau to suspect Sanders of being part of the movement, though she would need her friend's help.

"I'd rather not say," said Dana.

"You mean you can't do it," scoffed Charles.

"No, I just don't want to specify at this point and time. You said yourself that the council has been trying to get a spy into the resistance. What if he has been among you for a while?"

"What are you proposing?" asked Amy.

"Let me help with the uniforms and figure out how to get by the access codes. Don't worry. I'll deliver."

"You better," said Charles, "or this is all for naught."

"I will," said Dana.

"Alright," said Simon, "we'll trust you."

Relieved, Dana set about thinking of how she would get Sanders to break the codes without bringing him to the attention of Colonel Fernau.

"There isn't much else we can plan tonight," said Simon. "We will meet back here next week. George, you and Dana bring the uniforms. Dana, have those access codes broken."

"You got it, Simon," said George.

"Right then," said Simon. "See you all later. And be careful."

With the meeting ended, people left the building in twos so as not to attract attention. Dana and George left together. He guided her through the streets, taking extra precaution to avoid officers. Dana allowed herself to be led. She didn't know this area well and did not want to get lost.

Eventually, they reached the bus stop and Dana quickened her pace. "You got fare for the bus?" asked George.

Dana shook her head. She hadn't planned on taking the bus.

"Here," said George, handing her enough for one fare. "Don't worry. I have enough for me also."

The wheels of the bus squealed as it came to a screeching halt. Air blasted Dana as the doors opened. Dana stepped on board, putting her money into the machine. The bus driver eyed her curiously. Betraying nothing, Dana walked to the back and took a seat.

George paid his fare and took a seat in the middle. Dana frowned some with disappointment. Later, it occurred to her that George sat there on purpose so as not to alert anyone who might be watching that they came together. She settled into her seat and watched the lights streak past.

Giant screens lined the city with pictures of beautiful women and gorgeous men all dancing around. Their broad grins gave the impression that they were happy to be living in this world. Dana never witnessed any of that in real life.

The bus stopped at a light. Dana peeked out the window. Another screen with images and words sprang to life.

Help keep our society safe.

Dana read the words that popped on the screen.

Know anyone who is too individualistic?
See people gathering in secret?
Be aware of anyone who is unhappy or disagreeable.
Consult the nearest officer if you suspect something.

They are there to serve.

Yeah right, Dana thought. Officers were never friendly.

The bus jerked as it took off again. Ding! George had pressed the button, signaling that he wanted to get off. Instantly, the bus swerved to the right and stopped. Dana started to get up, but George shook his head slightly, telling her to stay out. She settled back down.

After a few more stops, the bus finally arrived at the one nearest the plant. Dana got off. Breathing deeply, she inhaled as much of the cold air as she could, relieved to be outside. The plant loomed before her. Dread filled Dana. She had no desire to go back.

Glancing around, Dana saw no sign of George. *Doesn't matter.* He knew that she could sneak in and out of the plant as she chose. Summoning her resolve, Dana headed back to her new life, her life as a spy for a man she detested.

CHAPTER

SEVENTEEN

"Sanders," said Dana approaching her friend, "may I have a word?"

"Yeah," replied Sanders, readjusting his glasses.

Dana pulled him to the side, away from prying eyes and overcurious ears. "I need a favor."

"What do you need?"

Dana covered the camera on her shirt with her hand, hoping that it would muffle what was said, if not eliminate it all together. "Do you know how the computers at the media center work?"

"Dana, where is this going?"

"Please, Sanders," pleaded Dana. "I need to know."

Sanders pulled her even further away from anyone who might be listening. "I get the feeling you are planning to do something stupid, if not dangerous."

"I have to. My par…" Dana stopped herself before she revealed anything more. "Lives depend on this. The media center."

Sanders leaned close. "The computers at the media center are locked with some sort of algorithm. They have firewall after firewall to keep anyone from hacking into the system. But it's not impenetrable."

Dana squeezed the button-sized camera even tighter, ignoring the discomfort of it digging into her skin.

"I can develop a program that will hack their system and put it on a disk for you."

"Will you?" Dana's relief came through in her voice.

"Dana, what is going on?" pushed Sanders.

"I can't tell you," the trepidation in her voice betrayed her.

"Dana." Sanders grabbed her arm, forcing her hand away from the concealed camera.

Instantly, Dana clasped her other hand around the camera, hoping that whoever watched didn't see Sanders' face or hear their conversation. She did not want to get him arrested.

"Please. Sanders, don't ask any questions. You can't help me."

"What do you mean?" asked Sanders.

"Just get me the decryption program by Wednesday. And don't ask why. It's better if you don't know."

Dana started to walk away. Sanders caught her arm. "I'll do it because you asked me to, but I can't help feeling that you're about to do something incredibly stupid."

"I don't have much choice."

Dana ran off before her emotions and guilt betrayed her. She raced to the locker room and locked herself inside. Her chest rose and fell rapidly as she breathed. Why, she asked herself, why must I be in this position?

Procuring the uniforms was not as difficult as Dana

had first thought. She and George had worked out the plan. With the help of Elsie, he would cause a distraction, while Dana snuck into the storage area with the uniforms.

Dana stood near the edge of the group on Outside Detail. She, George, and Elsie had managed to get on it for the same shift. Workers moved around, picking up bits of trash that blew off the trucks as they came in.

Dana spotted George. He nodded at her. *That's the signal.* Dana moved away from the group as they walked past the parked dump trucks.

George and Elsie approached one of the trucks. He hopped into the driver's seat and removed the brake. At the same instant, Elsie opened the hood and tossed in a homemade incendiary device. Quickly, they jumped away and blended in with the group.

The truck rolled down the hill, picking up speed as it went. Dana watched as it headed for a guard tower.

BOOM!

The explosion echoed all around them, reverberating off the buildings and surrounding hills. The force of the explosion knocked many off their feet. Debris flew everywhere, pelting officers and workers.

Dana took a quick glance at the half-gone tower. Not wasting any more time, she ran off. Slipping past the buildings and other officers unnoticed, Dana made her way to the storage building. Shouts and yells rose behind her as officers rounded people up and formed a line. Others headed for the smoldering remains of the truck. Dana ignored it all.

She found the building. Locked. She pulled out a pin and shoved it into the lock, moving it around until a familiar click registered. Hurriedly, Dana went inside. She glanced around at the various sections and what they held.

"Uniforms," she said to herself.

Dana perused the rows of items that the government did not trust them to recycle. She darted from section to section. Growing frustrated, Dana quickened her movements. She didn't have much time.

"There," she said to herself when she spotted the media uniforms.

Dana ran to them, but they were behind a chicken wire gate. Angered by this, she pulled out her pin and picked the lock. She rifled through them, looking for ones that were in good condition.

Officers walked by outside. Knowing her time grew short, Dana grabbed five uniforms, hoping that they were the right sizes. Clutching them, she replaced the lock on the gate and ran out the door.

Mad Dog stood there. Surprised, Dana stopped.

"Hurry up," said Mad Dog.

"How…"

"I saw you run. Now come on."

He pushed a cart to her. Dana plopped the uniforms in it, and together, they covered them with a tarp.

"Now go," said Mad Dog. "I'll take care of these."

Having little choice, Dana thanked Mad Dog and ran back to the burning truck, hoping she hadn't been tricked. She paused by the side of a building when she noticed the line of workers. Officer Burroughs read off the list of names.

Dana scanned the area. She needed to get in line before he reached her. She spotted Elsie. They locked eyes for a moment before Elsie waved her over. Glancing at the officers,

Dana seized her chance and darted for the line. She slipped in beside Elsie just as Officer Burroughs called her name.

"Dana Ginary," called Officer Burroughs.

"Here," said Dana, trying to control her breathing.

"Did you witness what happened?"

"No."

"Where were you when the truck exploded?" asked Officer Burroughs.

"Over there," said Dana, pointing to a spot.

Officer Burroughs eyed her suspiciously. "You seem out of breath."

"The excitement, sir."

"Sir," said another officer, walking up with the incendiary device. "This was in the engine."

Officer Burroughs took it, examining it carefully. "Who is responsible for this?" He held up the device.

No one spoke.

"I repeat, who is responsible for this?" Angered at the lack of response, Officer Burroughs paced before them. He pointed at various people, demanding if they knew anything. Each shook their heads.

Fuming, Officer Burroughs handed the device to one of his officers. "Since no one feels talkative, you will all remain out here until the one responsible comes forward."

Another man approached Officer Burroughs. Dana recognized him instantly as Colonel Fernau. He whispered into Officer Burroughs' ear for a minute.

"Everyone dismissed," barked Officer Burroughs when Colonel Fernau had finished speaking. "Get that truck out of here." He pointed at the burning dump truck as he marched away.

"What was that all about?" asked Elsie.

"Don't know," Dana lied. She turned and saw Colonel Fernau staring right at her, his gaze unnerving her. "Come on."

Dana steered Elsie away from the commotion, desperate to get away from the man.

Dana strolled through Shackville, relieved to be away from the confines of the plant and its ever watchful eyes. She hadn't visited Jesse in a long while and wished to see her. Trails of a breeze brushed her long, dark hair. A small group of children played with a ball. Admiring them, Dana wished she were that age again, an age where worry hadn't crossed paths with her.

One of the kids dropped the grungy ball. It rolled across the dirt and bumped against Dana's foot. She picked it up and tossed it to the waiting arms of the boy that had run after it. Sighing, she continued on.

The planned raid on the media center quickly approached. Dana wished she didn't have to go through with it. Thoughts of her parents locked away filled her mind. Swallowing back tears, she pushed open the door to Jesse's and let herself in.

"Good evening, dear," greeted Nana.

"Hello, Nana." Dana stomped the dirt from her boots.

"Dana!"

A squirt of red raced through the room, plowing into Dana. The two hugged each other for a long moment.

"Do your fish face," Jesse pleaded.

Dana knelt down on one knee to make herself level with Jesse. She sucked in her cheeks, narrowing her lips into a thin, vertical line. Squeals of laughter escaped Jesse. The girl's innocence and delight lifted Dana's spirits momentarily.

"Jesse," said Nana, "aren't you forgetting something."

Jesse's face scrunched up a bit as she thought about what she had forgotten. "Oh!"

Instantly, Jesse forced Dana into a chair. She rushed to the kitchen, and clamoring and clanking followed her. Like a whirlwind, the girl came back with a plate of dry toast and a glass of water.

"Here you go," said Jesse. "Eat and drink this."

Dana picked at the charred toast.

Laughing, Nana spoke. "Dear, you don't order them to eat. You just offer it to them."

"Oh," said Jesse. She snatched the toast from Dana's hand and held it out to her. "Would you like some toast? Here." Jesse plopped it back into Dana's lap.

"I'm trying to teach her hospitality," said Nana. "She hasn't quite gotten the hang of it. You don't need to eat it if you don't want to."

"It's fine." Dana nibbled on the toast. It tasted awful, but for Jesse's sake, she pretended to enjoy it. "The best toast I've ever had."

Jesse beamed with pride.

"How are things at the plant?" asked Nana.

"The same," said Dana. She put her plate down. "There haven't been any recent deaths."

"Good to hear."

Dana looked around the room. So much rested on her mind, pushing against her voice box to get out. She bit her tongue to keep silent.

"What is it, dear?" asked Nana.

"Nothing," muttered Dana. "Nana, have you ever had to do something you didn't want to? What I mean is, was there ever a time when you knew something was wrong, yet you did it to try and save someone you care about?"

"There are times when we all are forced to do things we don't want."

"Yes, but what if it goes beyond that?" Dana squeezed her hands together until they turned white. Her fidgeting did not go unnoticed.

"What is it, Dana?" Concern filled Nana's face.

"It's just… I…" Remembering the camera, Dana clammed up. "It's nothing. Forget I said anything."

Nana noticed Dana fiddling with the top button on her shirt. Her brows furrowed. "I don't know what's troubling you, but don't let it rob you of your soul."

"What do you mean?" asked Dana.

"We have a choice, Dana. When we are asked to do something, we have to decide if it is worth the price."

Dana's confused look told Nana that she did not understand. "I know it doesn't make sense right now, but someday it will."

"But what if no matter what you choose, someone gets hurt? What if there is no way to win?" asked Dana.

"You must make the right choice," said Nana.

"What if people die?"

"Dying doesn't mean that you've lost."

Dana glanced at Jesse, who had listened intently to their conversation. She wondered how much of it the girl understood. Jesse moved from her seat and nestled in Dana's lap, telling her that she understood more than people realized. Dana wrapped her arms around the child.

"You're lucky, you know," said Dana. "You two have each other."

The unspoken sentiment that even that would not last forever passed between them. No need in voicing what they already knew.

CHAPTER  EIGHTEEN

Dana pushed the crate back into place in front of the hole in the wall to the barracks. She stood up, turned around, and stopped cold, her heart leaping into her throat.

Colonel Fernau stood in front of her, wearing his crisp uniform. His fingers wrapped around the handle of his stick. Dana squirmed under his icy gaze.

"So the mystery of how you manage to come and go has been explained," he said.

Dana did not care for his sarcastic tone. She had a feeling that he always knew. "Where is everyone?"

"On an emergency drill."

Dana looked around the empty barracks, desperately wishing it were filled with anyone but Colonel Fernau.

"I grow tired of waiting," said Colonel Fernau.

"I... I..."

"By now, you should know who the leaders of the resistance are."

"There have only been two meetings."

"And who seemed to be in charge?"

Dana didn't answer.

"Come now, Miss Ginary."

"A man named Simon and one named Charles," relented Dana. Guilt gnawed at her.

"And your friend George?"

"He is just a nobody."

"I don't believe that and neither do you."

"He doesn't make the decisions," said Dana.

"But he has influence."

"I don't know."

"Miss Ginary, do you want your parents dead?"

Dana gaped at Colonel Fernau and his suggestion.

"I don't blame you if you do. They are a burden. Your father has developed a nasty cough, and considering our limited resources, I very much doubt that he will receive treatment. No, perhaps we have been pushing the wrong button."

Sweat formed on Dana's neck.

"You visited that girl again, didn't you? Perhaps I should pay her a visit as well."

"No!" Dana recoiled after her outburst. "Please, I don't know much. You've been watching on the camera. You know what they have planned."

"Yes, about that." Colonel Fernau picked up an item of clothing from a bunk and tossed it aside. "Interesting thing about that camera. Seems to get covered up at times. I don't want to accuse you of anything, but it's almost as though you are trying to hide something."

Dana backed against the wall. She wished she had thought about the fact that they might have been watching very closely.

"I've told the First Councilman that it was simply an oversight on your part." Colonel Fernau approached until his face practically touched Dana's. Surprisingly, his breath smelled of peppermint. "Don't let it happen again."

Dana nodded.

"When is your little raid on the media center supposed to take place?"

"I—I don't know. I won't know until the day it's supposed to happen."

Colonel Fernau studied Dana. "Find a way to let us know. We will, of course, be waiting."

Colonel Fernau's polished boots clicked on the floor as he left. Dana released a huge breath, relieved to be free of him for the moment. She slumped against the wall, wishing it was all over.

CHAPTER NINETEEN

Once again, Dana found herself working in the incinerator. She wiped her forehead with the back of her glove, the rough fibers scratching her skin. She leaned on her rake a bit, resting from the work, her tired muscles desperate for relief.

"Get back to work!"

An officer waved his baton at her. Immediately, Dana lifted her rake and pushed more junk into the flames. *Bastard.* She would have loved to see one of them working for a change.

George came up beside her. "Keep working," he said. "Tonight."

"Huh?"

"It's tonight," repeated George. "Simon says that tonight is the night. Be at the media center by nine. Bring the uniforms. And take the bus."

"Will you be there?"

"Yeah, but I'm arriving another way."

A bad feeling wafted over her. "George," said Dana, covering the camera. She no longer cared if anyone watched. "I don't think you should go."

"Why not?"

"Please. I have a bad feeling."

"Now don't you worry," said George. "We've been through this. Nothing is going to happen."

"George, please"

"I suggest you worry about yourself." George tapped her chin affectionately before going back to his work.

Despair filled Dana. She wished she could tell him. Resigned that she was about to commit the most heinous of sins, Dana continued her tasks, counting the hours until 9 p.m.

When the buzzer rang, she put her rake and gloves away, filing into the eating hall with everyone else. Dana shuffled along. She picked up a tray and allowed the server to plop a bowl of orange goo on it. She sometimes wondered if they purposefully changed the color of the food just to make things more interesting.

"Orange today," said Elsie as she sat beside Dana. "At least it doesn't look like vomit. Well, not too much anyway."

Dana picked at her food. She placed spoonfuls in her mouth, not even tasting it.

"What's the matter?"

"Nothing," said Dana. "Just tired."

"I did it!" said Sanders, a bit too loud for Dana's taste.

"Did what?" asked Elsie.

"My best work ever," said Sanders, pulling out a disk the size of his thumb.

Dana covered the camera again. She may not be able to save George, but she could try to keep Sanders and Elsie out of it.

"Here," Sanders handed Dana the disk. It was attached to a chain so she could wear it around her neck. "I have successfully created the only series of logarithms and viruses that can break any decryption code and firewall. You plug that into any government computer, and in about 30 seconds, you will be in its mainframe. Booyah!"

"Keep it down," said Elsie, pulling Sanders back into his chair. "And why are you trying to break into government computers?"

"I asked him to," said Dana.

"What?"

"Please, just trust me on this." Once again, tears welled in her eyes as she thought about her parents. "I have to do something tonight. Something big. And I need you two to not ask questions, because if things go wrong—please, my parents' lives depend on this."

"Fine," said Elsie.

"Oh," said Sanders, "Mad Dog wanted me to tell you that the stuff is under your bunk. Do you know what that is about?"

Dana noticed Officer Burroughs heading straight for her. Fearful that he suspected she told them everything, she jumped from her seat and ran off.

Elsie watched, putting together what frightened Dana. As Officer Burroughs walked by, she pushed her tray off the table and towards him. A loud crash garnered everyone's attention. Orange goo covered Officer Burroughs' pants. He glared at her.

Slap!

Elsie clutched the side of her face that stung and bore a red mark from where she had been struck.

"Stupid girl," grumbled Officer Burroughs. He stalked off.

Elsie looked in the direction Dana had run, pleased that her friend had managed to get away for the moment.

Dana burst into the barracks. She ran straight for her bunk and pulled out a bag that Mad Dog had hidden underneath it, containing the uniforms. Quickly, she changed into street clothes. Her work plant outfit would be a dead giveaway that she didn't belong. Zipping up her jacket, Dana snatched the bag and her money and left.

"Oomph!"

She had run right into Mad Dog.

"What's your hurry?" he asked. "Oh, it's you."

"Thanks," said Dana.

"Don't mention it. Ever," replied Mad Dog.

Dana decided to take a chance that he might help her again. "Officer Burroughs is on his way here," she said, gambling on the universal hatred for the man. "I need you to keep him busy so I can get away."

"What'd you do?"

"Uh, you'll find out soon," said Dana. "Look, if you want to get even with me for breaking your nose…"

"Naw, that's in the past. Besides, I owe him a few favors." Mad Dog cracked his knuckles. He had been on the receiving end of Officer Burroughs' anger too many times. "Go on. Get out of here. My friends and I will take care of Officer Burroughs."

"Thanks."

Dana ran out the door and to the outside world. She

hurried down the hill to the fence, not caring if any of the officers saw her. She couldn't wait until nine o'clock. Once at the fence, she squeezed through, making certain her bag did not snag on the barbs.

Racing down the hill, Dana knew she could wait at Jesse's until it was time to take the bus. She stopped. *I can't wait there and endanger them.* Veering to the left, Dana decided to just go straight to the tracks. She would just wait around there. Few guards patrolled the area, since only freight trains came through there.

Her feet slid on the gravel as she charged downhill. Losing her balance, Dana threw her hands out to catch herself. She jumped back to her feet and continued on, ignoring the bruises she had acquired.

A lone cart sat in the fading sunlight. Dana hopped on it and worked the mechanism to move it. She powered the thing, pushing it toward the city. Thankful for the darkness that settled around her, she slipped by a few officers who had snuck out for a smoking break, a violation of the law, since all tobacco had been banned.

Dana ignored the chilly wind that ripped past her, flinging her hair everywhere. Panting, she pushed onward. Her muscles burned from the effort. *Keep going.* Not allowing herself a chance to rest, she worked even harder to reach the edges of the city.

As more lights came into view, Dana knew she had gone far enough. She slowed the cart and hopped off. Quickly, Dana found a spot within view of the bus stop. She settled down, placing the pack in her lap as she waited for the hours to pass until the time had come for her to catch the bus.

~ ~ ~

"Sanders," hissed Elsie. "Where are you going?"

Sanders crept through the hallways, heading straight for Officer Burroughs' office. Word had spread that the plant commandant had met with some unfortunate accident and was locked in a freezer that no one could open.

Using the opportunity, Sanders decided to learn what had bothered Dana the last few weeks. He peeked around a corner and found an officer leaning back in her chair at her desk. The stifled yawn told him she had been there too long and wished to leave.

"Sanders."

"Shush," he silenced Elsie. "Dana has been acting weird lately, you know that. I intend to find out why."

"By sneaking into Officer Burroughs' office?"

"Why do you think she was in such a hurry to get away from him?"

Elsie relented. "How do you propose we get by her?"

Sanders thought a moment. He grabbed a tack from the bulletin board above him. Taking careful aim, he threw it at the woman. It clinked against the side of her desk.

Startled, the woman sat upright. She glanced around the room, her eyes scanning every detail.

Sanders snatched another tack. Carefully, he chucked it to the other side of the room.

Clink! Clink!

The woman rose to her feet. She moved slowly across the room to where the noise had come from. Searching around, the female officer never noticed as Sanders and Elsie raced to Officer Burroughs' office. They slipped inside and quietly closed the door.

"This is completely insane," whispered Elsie.

"Just keep a lookout," said Sanders, running to the computer. He brought up the holographic monitor.

"Are you sure you can break the passcode—oh." Elsie stopped speaking when the screen flicked to the desktop home. "Sanders, you're a genius."

"I know."

Sanders' fingers flew over the keyboard as he pulled up file after file, searching for anything that might shed light on Dana's behavior. Window after window popped up, allowing him to quickly scan it before moving to the next one.

"What's that?" Elsie pointed to a file on the screen.

Sanders brought it up. Instantly, the interrogation of Dana opened up. Sanders turned on the audio.

Do you miss your parents? It would be unfortunate if they never returned home.

What are you saying?

Cold sweat covered both Elsie and Sanders as they listened.

"She's going to betray the resistance," said Sanders.

"She's being forced to," said Elsie. "Now it all makes sense. No wonder she didn't want to be around us. She was trying to protect us."

Sanders dug around in search of a disk.

"What are you doing?" asked Elsie.

"Making copies," said Sanders as he found one, shoved it into the slot, and pressed save. He pulled out the disk and jammed another into the slot. "I'm making a lot of copies."

~ ~ ~

The gurgling engine of the bus as it neared alerted Dana that the hour had arrived. She sprinted from her spot and ran to the bus stop, arriving just in time to board.

"Almost didn't make it, missy," said the driver.

Dana smiled and put her fare into the slot. Glad that the bus was close to full, Dana found an empty seat and sat down. She glanced at the other faces around her. None of them looked in her direction. Most stared at their laps or blankly out the window.

Sighing heavily, Dana focused on the objects whizzing by the window. Her heart pounded against her ribcage. She feared that at any moment, it might burst through her chest.

The bus stopped at a red light. Dana glanced up at the giant TV screen above her. Once again, it warned of people who were too independent.

Together, we are stronger. Alone, you are vulnerable.

Bullshit, thought Dana, you're alone even when you're part of a group. She had never felt more alone. A plume of black smog escaped the tailpipe of the bus as it shifted into gear.

Dana remembered being told once that the individual ownership of vehicles had been banned because of limited resources and environmental concerns. She counted the number of cars on the road, thinking back to all the times she had to ride the smoky dump truck while picking up garbage around the city. *Funny how cars were banned for the environment, and yet there are an awful lot of them on the road.* A limousine passed the bus. Rage filled Dana. She remembered her grandfather telling her and her sister about the time he was her age and had a car. One day, government officials took it, saying that a law was passed, making it illegal to own cars. Since then, she never knew anyone that personally owned one. *So who owns all these?*

A bump in the road jostled her from her thoughts. *Pay attention to your mission.* She continued looking out the window, always mindful of where the bus was at.

There it is!

Dana pushed the button, and the driver pulled the bus over to the curb. She hopped out the back door, clutching her bag tightly. Noting where the officers were, Dana trotted down the street toward the media center. She kept the collar of her jacket up, doing her best to conceal her face.

Finely dressed people passed by her. They laughed and joked among themselves. Seeing their tags, Dana knew they worked within the Council Building itself. Such people always enjoyed more freedom than others.

Dana spotted an officer coming towards her. She turned a corner and quickened her pace. If stopped, one scan of the chip in her arm would reveal she didn't belong. Only certain people were allowed into the city at night. Others, like her, were forced to stay in. Besides, she wasn't even supposed to be outside the plant.

Dana turned another corner, circling back to the media center. The officer had gone. She hurried to her destination before another showed up. Despite the chill, Dana sweated profusely, causing her shirt to cling to her back and itch.

Almost there.

She hoped George had not made it out of the plant. Her hopes were quickly dashed when a hand reached out and seized her, yanking her into a back alley.

"What…" a hand covered her mouth.

"Shh," said George, "it's me."

Crestfallen, Dana looked at him. Once again, she wanted to tell him to run, but the thought of her parents at the mercy of Colonel Fernau stopped her.

"This way." George pulled her along. They darted through stagnant puddles and to the far end of the building where the staff door and the others were.

"Got them?" asked Charles.

Dana studied the faces around her. She recognized Amy, Charles, Simon, and George. There was only one she didn't know, another female who looked as though she worked in the media center.

She tossed the bag to Charles. "The uniforms are in there," she said as she pulled out the chain around her neck with the disk, "and this is the decryption disk."

"Everyone suit up," said Simon.

The people around her put on a media center technician uniform from Dana's bag. She put one on as well, pulling it up over her clothes.

"Ready?" asked the woman Dana didn't know.

"Yes," said Simon.

The female employee swiped her ID badge and let them inside. Once again, Dana entered an unfamiliar world. Lush couches, easy chairs, and polished tables lined the hallways and offices. Jealousy gripped her again. She pushed it out of her mind. *No time for that.*

They moved quickly through the empty building and its sparse lighting. Dana peeked in the rooms as they passed, noting the high-tech equipment in all of them. Their feet made swift rustling sounds as they trotted across the carpet.

The woman scanned her badge at a heavy, steel door and opened it. Quickly, everyone moved through the opening and into a stairwell.

"Charles, you remain here at the front. If anything happens, pull the fire alarm. The rest of us will go to the top floor where the mainframe is," said Simon.

Charles nodded and took his position, hoisting his gun. "Don't take too long."

Simon clasped his friend on the shoulder. He charged up the stairs, followed by the others. Their feet clopped on the linoleum as they raced up the steps to the top floor. Once reaching it, the woman with the badge swiped it and pulled the door open.

"Quickly," she said.

Dana ran into the dark room with the others. Her mind raced over telling everyone the truth or just running away.

"Dana, the disk," said Simon as he sat in front of a holographic monitor and clicked it on. She handed him the disk and he started to put it into the slot.

Clap. Clap. Clap.

Everyone whirled around to see who clapped their hands. Lights flickered on, revealing a bunch of armed officers and Colonel Fernau. He walked up to them with a triumphant smile, his hands squeezed tightly around his stick.

"I commend you all on managing to get inside." Colonel Fernau stopped in front of Dana. "You are to be congratulated for your efforts."

"Congratulated?" said George. "Dana, what is he talking about?"

Dana stared at the floor in shame.

"Oh, yes. It appears you have a traitor in your midst,"

sneered Colonel Fernau. "Dana here was simply doing my bidding. I needed to find the leaders of the resistance, and she willingly helped."

Tears filled Dana's eyes as she continued to stare at the floor.

"Don't be shy, dear." Colonel Fernau lifted her chin with his stick. "Take pride in what you have done."

The faces looking back at her tore at her heart. Disgust and loathing wafted over her, filling her every being.

"And you." Colonel Fernau walked over to the woman who had the ID badge. "You despicable creature. You were once a decorated officer of Dystopia, and now you are here with them. Their lies have corrupted even the officers."

"I'm not the one spreading lies," hissed the woman.

Swiftly, Colonel Fernau pulled out his pistol and shot the woman in the head. Her body slumped to the floor, forming a pool of blood.

Horrified, Dana just stared at the woman's corpse.

"Take this rabble away," said Colonel Fernau, putting his gun away.

Officers seized the people around Dana. George elbowed one and attempted to flee. Ruthlessly, Colonel Fernau whipped out his stick, striking George in the face and knocking him down. He raised his stick again.

"Stop!" Dana's voice quieted the room.

Colonel Fernau gave her a menacing glare, but lowered his switch. "Get them out of here!"

The armed officers filed everyone out of the room.

"I don't blame you for what you did," said Simon to Dana as he walked by.

The sincerity in his voice choked her. Unshakable guilt filled her heart as she watched those who trusted her, those whom she called friends, being led away by the very people she despised.

Dana snatched the disk Sanders had given her before anyone else could. She put it around her neck and tucked it under her shirt. A glint of gold caught her eye. Curious, Dana reached down and picked it up. George's locket. Realizing he must have lost it when Colonel Fernau struck him, Dana put it around her neck as well and tucked it under her shirt.

"Miss Ginary." Colonel Fernau stood in the doorway waiting for her.

Grudgingly, Dana moved and walked with him down the stairs. His obviously fake smile unnerved her.

Once outside, Dana noticed Charles being pushed into an armored truck with the others. They must have gotten him earlier, she thought. Not knowing where to go, Dana stopped on the sidewalk.

"Miss Ginary," said Colonel Fernau, holding the door to a limousine open for her and waving her in.

She did not like his sudden niceness. Not wanting to cause trouble, Dana stepped into the limousine and sat down. Seth Michaels and Kenny were already in there. Colonel Fernau sat beside her.

"Well done, my girl," said Seth Michaels in an exuberant voice. "What we have been trying to do for ages, you managed to do within weeks. This is truly a day to remember."

"Yes," said Colonel Fernau. "Drink?" He held out a glass with a gold, sparkling liquid that Dana had never seen before.

Unsure of what to do, she accepted the offer. Dana took a sip. The bubbles tickled her throat as they went down. Deciding she did not like this beverage, she placed the glass to one side.

"How are my parents?" asked Dana.

"They're fine, dear," Seth Michaels waved her question away.

"When may I see them?"

"Soon."

Dana did not care for his evasiveness.

The limo meandered down the street, passing the armored truck when it stopped in front of the Detention Center. She watched as the others were shoved into the building, knowing full well what their fate would be. Once again, guilt panged her.

"What's the matter, Dana?" said Seth Michaels. "You seem down."

"Just tired," Dana said quickly. "Too much excitement."

"Ah, yes, well, when we get back, you and your parents can take a long rest."

Colonel Fernau and Seth Michaels exchanged knowing glances. Ill feeling filled Dana.

"But for now, there are things that must be done," said Colonel Fernau.

The limousine pulled to a halt outside a building.

"My office is in here," said Seth Michaels. "One of the officers will take you there, where you may rest for the moment."

The door opened and an officer held his gloved hand out for Dana. Unused to such treatment, she took it, warily allowing the man to help her out of the car.

"It will only be for a moment," Seth Michaels reassured her as she stepped through the glass doors.

CHAPTER TWENTY

Sanders and Elsie both stared at the computer screen, watching events as they unfolded. Sanders had hacked the surveillance cameras. Glued to the monitor, they observed as Dana and the others were led away by the officers.

"What is going on?" asked Elsie.

"Nothing good," said Sanders.

His fingers zipped over the keyboard, bringing up screen after screen with all sorts of nonsensical writing. After several minutes, he closed them and clicked open another window with live feed coming from the cameras in the building containing the First Councilman's office.

"What are you doing?" asked Elsie.

Sanders smiled as he readjusted his glasses. "I have a little surprise planned for our friends."

"What surprise?"

"You'll see."

Sanders hunched over the screen, watching every move that the officers and Dana made. He turned up the audio so he could listen.

"Revenge of the geek," Sanders muttered to himself.

Elsie gave him an odd look.

Scuffling sounds echoed from beyond the door. Frightened, Elsie gripped Sanders' shoulder while he clasped the armrests of the chair. Slowly, the door opened as the hinges creaked in tune with their pounding hearts.

Mad Dog poked his head in.

Both Elsie and Sanders sighed with relief.

"What are you doing here?" asked Elsie, unsure of whether he would turn them in or not.

"Sneaking around like you," replied Mad Dog. "You know, you two really need to learn how to post a lookout. The lady officer almost walked right in here."

Elsie peeked around Mad Dog and noticed the still form of the officer.

"Don't worry. She's only unconscious."

"Where's Officer Burroughs?" asked Elsie.

"Still in the kitchen freezer," replied Mad Dog. "Locked in."

"Not for long, once they find the key," muttered Sanders.

"You mean this key?" Mad dog held up a ring of keys and jiggled them before tossing them aside. "Besides, I melted the lock."

"How?" asked both Elsie and Sanders.

"A little bit of gunpowder and heat."

Elsie laughed. "I knew one day your pyrotechnic ways would prove useful. So, you're not turning us in?"

"Depends on what you're doing."

"Hacking into the government's media network and surveillance cameras," said Sanders. He spouted off a few technical terms, but no one understood them.

"Causing trouble," said Elsie, "and trying to help Dana."

"Then I'm in." Mad Dog shut the door and moved closer.

Elsie studied him. "You don't even like Dana."

Mad Dog fingered the scar on his neck that Officer Burroughs had given him. "I like them even less."

Together, Elsie and Mad Dog leaned over Sanders as he whizzed through the computer system, muttering technical jargon to himself.

"Just ignore it," said Elsie when she noticed Mad Dog's confused look. "Half the time, I never know what he's saying."

"It's done," said Sanders. "Let's get out of here."

"What's done?" asked Mad Dog.

"In about 20 minutes, all of Dystopia will be watching the series of videos I just put together," replied Sanders. "We do not want to be here when it happens."

"Uh, Sanders," said Elsie, "won't they trace the uplink to this computer?"

"Precisely."

"This is Officer Burroughs' computer," said Elsie.

"And he will have a lot of explaining to do later," replied Sanders.

Mad Dog chuckled. "Yo, dawg, I wish I knew you while I was in school."

"Let's go."

They hurried out of the office, closing the door behind them and allowing the lock to latch. Carefully, they crept out of the office area and back to the main part of the plant.

~ ~ ~

Dana paced the office of Kenny's father impatiently. *What is taking so long?* Something did not seem right, but when she opened the door to leave, an officer told her to remain inside. Feeling like a prisoner, Dana forced the raging thoughts in her head to a standstill.

"You are to be congratulated," said Colonel Fernau as he walked into the room.

Dana remained silent. She did not feel worth the praise, even if it was false praise.

"Of course, this means that you are a hero as you have helped to locate the resistance," continued Colonel Fernau.

"My parents," whispered Dana.

Colonel Fernau stared at her with cold, unfeeling eyes.

"I was told that if I helped you locate the resistance that my parents would be released," said Dana.

"And so they shall," said Kenny's father as he entered the room. "In time. Colonel, a word."

Colonel Fernau stepped out of the room, leaving Dana alone. She stood up to stretch her cramped muscles, her movements bumping the desk and flicking the computer monitor on. Curious, Dana moved for a closer look. Her parents' pictures were on the screen.

Dana clicked on her father's. The word "terminated" in red letters stretched across it. She clicked on her mother's.

Terminated.

Horrorstruck, Dana realized that she had been lied to and that she foolishly believed the lies. She noticed her picture on the screen. She clicked on it.

Subject to termination.

The door shuffled open. Immediately, Dana clicked off the monitor and stepped away from the desk.

"You will come with me," said Colonel Fernau.

Dana followed the man through the hallway and its menacing fluorescent lights. The booming of a microphone and speakers grew louder and louder as they climbed a stairwell.

"Where are we going?" asked Dana.

"To your reward," answered Colonel Fernau. "You are a hero. The woman who brought down the resistance. All of Dystopia will hail your deed."

Doors opened before them as Dana was pushed onto a grand stage with decorations, gigantic television screens, balloons, and confetti. Seth Michaels spoke into the microphone, with Halloway standing next to him. Kenny stood toward the back. Dana walked up behind him, noting the way he beamed at her.

"Congratulations," Kenny hugged her.

Dana remained stiff.

"What is the matter?" asked Kenny.

"Kenny," Dana said softly. "Did you know that your father had already had my parents murdered?"

Kenny stepped back with a confused look on his face. His father's voice echoed around them from the speakers hanging directly above.

"Did you know that I was to be gotten rid of as well?" continued Dana.

"No..."

"You're such a liar, Kenny."

"And I give you," continued Seth Michaels, "the girl who

delivered the band of traitors and the man who led them, who meant to harm you all. I give you Dana Ginary, the savior of Dystopia!"

A hand pressed against Dana's back, shoving her to the front of the stage where Kenny's father stood with Halloway. They both shook her hand, giving her a series of congratulations before handing her the microphone.

Dana stood frozen, staring out at the mass of faces looking up at her with smiles and gleeful expressions, all expecting her to make a speech. They disgusted her. If only they knew how her parents were murdered and she was used.

"Thank you," said Dana. "First Councilman. When you first came to me with your proposal, I was hardly in a position to refuse."

The man's brow arched.

Dana continued. "But I want to extend to you my gratitude for giving me the opportunity to learn what Dystopia is all about and what values are honored here. Lying, cheating, coercion, the elimination of one's rights, murder, and the betrayal of one's friends."

Dana stole a quick glance at Kenny.

"These are what make Dystopia and our illustrious president great." Dana looked up at the poster of President Klens posed as though she reigned supreme above all of them. "These are the chains we have shackled ourselves with. Enjoy your servitude to the First Councilman and the president!"

Dana stared defiantly into the fuming eyes of Kenny's father as he glared at her with pure hatred. She dropped the microphone and walked off the stage amidst the stunned silence. Colonel Fernau attempted to grab her. Bringing her fist back, Dana rammed it into his nose, feeling it crack. She burst through the metal doors and into a long, empty hallway just as the video of her interrogation flickered onto the giant screen.

She knew where George and the others were being kept. She knew what she had to do.

Dana ran down the hallway. She stopped short when she noticed a locker room with uniforms hanging up on a rack. Whistling filled the area as one officer showered. Quickly, Dana stole into the room. She snatched one of the uniforms and put it on. A knife caught her eye. Dana looked at her forearm. *The chip.* She knew they could track her with it.

She clicked open the switchblade. Gritting her teeth, Dana plunged the steel of the knife into her flesh and dug out the chip. Once it popped out, she wrapped a towel around her arm and pulled her sleeve over it. A janitor walked past with a cart, humming a merry tune. Acting as though she belonged, Dana marched past him, dropping her chip onto his cart.

She raced through the hall and down the stairs, bursting through the door that led outside. Hurriedly, Dana bolted down the sidewalk. The Detention Center wasn't far. Ignoring the odd glances she received, Dana ran as fast as she could. Many jumped out of her way, afraid of being detained themselves. She rushed past them.

Pausing, Dana recalculated her route to the Detention Center. She charged down an alley, coming out on the other side. Making a right, she ran for the building where George was being held. Slowing down, Dana caught her breath. She approached the doors of the center. Locked. She pressed the call button. The man at the front desk looked at her and clicked a button on his end.

"Yes?" his voice crackled on the speaker.

Dana didn't answer.

"Name and ID please," said the man.

Looking through the glass doors, Dana shook her head as though she didn't hear him.

"Damn fools," muttered the man at the desk. "They told me they fixed it."

He pulled out his key card and unlocked the front doors. "May I help you?"

Instantly, Dana jabbed the man in the neck so he couldn't talk. She shoved him back, shut the door, and locked it. Turning back around, Dana knocked the man unconscious. She looked around. No one. Heaving the man up, Dana propped him in his chair so it would look like he had fallen asleep. She knew the ruse wouldn't work for long.

She clicked on the computer screen. Scanning the list of new detainees, she quickly spotted George's name. "Cell block five," she whispered to herself. "Where's cell block five?"

Dana spotted a map pinned to the wall. Not having time to memorize it, she yanked it down and took it with her. She sped through the hallway to the elevator. According to the map, she needed to go down two floors.

The elevator dinged as it stopped on her floor. She heard voices on the other side. Swiftly, she darted behind a group of plants and hunkered low. Two officers stepped out of the elevator going in the direction away from her, ignorant of her presence.

Relieved, Dana dashed into the elevator before the doors closed. She pushed the button for Basement Level 2. It crept downward at a snail's pace, causing Dana to grow more impatient.

Ding!

The doors slid open. Dana bolted out. Reading the map, she darted to the left and sped down the dimly lit hallway. Her boots made clacking sounds as she went. Skidding to a halt, Dana paused as the hallway split into two directions.

Right.

She ran off. Dana sped past doors and rooms to where she knew she had to go. She checked the map again. *Almost there.* Despite the ache in her muscles, Dana hurried to cell block five.

There it is!

She ran to the door. A man's laughter spilled from it. Halting, Dana regained her composure. She had to think of something and it had to be believable. Straightening her collar and her hair, Dana walked in with a regal posture.

"You there," she tried to sound authoritative. "What is the meaning of this?"

The man snapped to attention. He snatched his hat and rammed it on his head.

A quick scan of the room told Dana that he had been watching contraband videos. "You know these videos are banned. And sloughing on the job. The captain won't be happy to hear this."

"No, ma'am," said the officer. "Please don't report me."

"I might be willing to let it slide just this once," Dana paced the room getting into the role. "Clean this stuff up and throw it in the dumpster outside. And don't let me catch you like this again."

The frightened officer pulled the videos out of the player and ran out of the room. Dana rushed to the individual cells. "George?"

No answer.

"George," she said more loudly.

"Dana?"

Dana rushed to the cell the voice came from. "George! Come on. Let's go."

She used the key card she had taken from the man at the desk to open the cell. Dana noticed that Amy, Simon, and Charles were in the next cell. She opened it as well.

"What are you doing here, Dana?" asked George.

"Rescuing you," replied Dana as though it should have been obvious.

"Another trick I suppose," muttered Charles.

"Please," pleaded Dana. "I am sorry for what happened. They had my parents and if I hadn't…" Dana broke off. "It didn't matter anyway."

Silence ensued. The others had figured out what had happened.

"How do we know we can trust you now?" asked Amy.

Dana looked into their faces, time running short. Knowing only one way to convince them, she pulled up her sleeve and held out her arm. They all looked at the bloodied cloth she had wrapped around it.

"You pulled out your chip," said Amy.

"It's enough for me," said George, stepping out of his cell.

The others followed. Together, they all ran out of the room and for the elevator. Dana pushed the button. Impatiently, they waited for the familiar bell that signaled the elevator had arrived. Once the doors opened, they scrambled inside and hit the button for the lobby.

"They'll know we have escaped soon," said Simon.

As though to prove his point, the alarm sounded. Red lights and blaring sirens alerted everyone to the breakout.

"All right," said Simon. "We'll split up. All of us will go

our separate ways and meet up later. You know where. If you don't show, we'll assume the worse."

"I'm going with Dana," said George. "She doesn't know where the place is. And I suspect it's her they want most at this point."

"Very well," Simon agreed.

The elevator stopped and the doors opened. They hurried from it, running straight for the exit. Despite the alarms blaring, no one guarded it. All of them burst through the glass doors and into the street, each heading in a different direction.

George grabbed Dana's arm and pulled her along. She allowed him to guide her. "We need to get out of the city."

"Where?"

"The tracks," said George as they ran. "There are usually freight trains that leave at about this time. We'll hop on one and take it out of Dystopia."

They ran down the sidewalk away from the Detention Center.

"You there!" shouted an officer at them.

Cursing at being spotted, Dana ran faster. She noticed that the officer spoke into his radio, summoning more troops. George veered to the right. Dana followed. More officers waited for them. Quickly, George jerked her to the left. They darted down an alley, splashing through the muddy water that pooled there. Coming out the other side, the two made a quick turn and ran fast.

Sirens blared behind them. Knowing they would soon be cornered if they remained on foot, Dana seized George's arm and pulled him behind a building. They waited in the shadows, watching as officers gathered and spoke to one another.

"Could they be tracking your chip?" asked Dana.

"Nope. Dug mine out years ago."

The officers turned their backs. Quickly, they dashed from their hiding spot and bolted down the street, blending in with the crowd as best they could.

"There they go!"

Gun shots rang out as armed officers opened fire. Many people screamed and dropped to the ground. Dana and George continued running.

Dana noticed George slowing down, clutching his side. She grabbed his arm and pulled him onward. "Lean on me."

Together, they jogged down the street, taking another turn. George's heavy breaths worried Dana. Blood poured from his wound. Spotting a row of vehicles, Dana steered them to it. She cruised down the line of cars with George on her arm. Quickly, she peeked in each window looking for one with the keys inside. Her luck rested with an abandoned pickup truck.

It opened when she touched the handle. Without losing a beat, Dana put George on the passenger side and hurried to the driver's seat. The key lay in the ignition.

The truck gurgled and spurted to life as the engine turned over. Jamming the thing into first gear, she punched the accelerator. The truck frogged a bit as Dana coordinated her feet to work the clutch.

"Do you know how to drive one of these?" coughed George.

"Sort of," said Dana.

She had never driven a vehicle before. Once, when she was 13, her father explained the mechanics of driving as it had been explained to him by her grandfather. She had watched the drivers of the dump truck many times and knew how it was supposed to work. As for actually operating one, this was her first time.

Despite the jerky movements, Dana managed to get the truck to go forward. She shifted into second and then third gear. Speeding down the street, she had hoped they wouldn't be noticed. Her mood dropped when she came upon a line of officer cars. Colonel Fernau stood in front of them with a murderous look in his eyes. Somehow, he had read her intentions.

Dana stomped on the brakes. Ramming the truck into reverse, she peeled the pavement as she backed up, shifted into first, and took off. With each movement, Dana became more familiar with the truck.

Careening down the street, Dana wove in and out of traffic, barely missing the cars around her. She scraped the side of a convertible. Shifting up, Dana rammed her foot on the accelerator, heading outside the city.

Cars pursued her. Their sirens and peels of gunfire told her that getting out of the city was easier said than done. Dana veered to the left. The back wheels skidded and she had to hang onto the wheel, turning into the skid to avoid spinning out. Once she had straightened out, she sped up.

George moaned beside her. The pool of blood on his shirt grew larger.

"You with me over there?" said Dana.

"I'm still here. Side hurts like hell though."

She noted the pale look on his face. They had to get away.

Dana slammed on the brakes. Instantly, she rammed the truck into reverse and punched the throttle. Driving backwards and trying not to hit anyone, Dana maneuvered the truck through the line of cars that chased her. Once past, she spun around and sped down an alley. Using the alleys to hike through the city, Dana neared the edge.

The horn of a train alerted her that they were close.

"We need to ditch this truck," panted George.

Dana agreed. Once they had the tracks in sight, she parked the truck next to another. Jumping out, Dana rushed to the passenger side. Carefully, she helped George stand up, wrapping his arm around her shoulder. Blood from his wound spilled onto her shirt. Ignoring it, Dana half carried, half dragged him down the hill to the train.

Dancing light in the distance caught her attention. Pausing, Dana looked in the direction of the plant. The entire area seemed to be ablaze. "Jesse," she whispered.

"I'm sure she got out all right," said George.

The screeching of tires and blaring sirens forced her to move. Dana clung to George as they ran for the train yard. More gunfire whizzed by them.

"Stop her!" yelled Colonel Fernau as he stepped out of his car.

Dana pushed harder. They couldn't stop. George leaned heavily on her, slowing her down.

"You must go on without me," he coughed.

"No," said Dana, "I left you behind once. I'm not doing it again."

She took them down a line of crates. Taking a chance, Dana put George down. "Rest a moment. They're tied up on the hill."

Thankful, George allowed himself to be put on the ground.

Dana studied the freight trains. She found one pointed west. Knowing that that one would take them away from the city, she kept a careful eye on it.

George's coughing distracted her. Dana took off her jacket and placed it on his bullet wound. "Here," she said, pulling off the locket and handing it to him. "You dropped this."

George's blood-stained hand grasped the locket. He

rubbed his thumb over it before giving it back to Dana. "Keep it. It's yours now."

The squeals of train wheels and shouts of officers snapped Dana back to the present. "Come on." She lifted George up again.

Together, they hopped over tracks and past parked trains as they made their way to the one that had started moving.

"There they are!"

Dana quickened her pace. She held tightly to George, determined not to let him go. His head bobbed a bit, his breathing more labored than before.

"Almost there," Dana encouraged him.

With renewed vigor, George picked up his pace to match Dana's. They reached the moving train. Scanning the cars, Dana found one with an open door. She and George ran beside it.

"You first," said George.

Dana reached out, grasped the bar on the side of the car, and heaved herself inside. Her side throbbed a bit as she landed on the hard surface. Whirling around, Dana reached her hand out for George. He had lagged behind.

"George!" yelled Dana. "George, come on!"

Dana leaned out as far as she could, reaching for her friend. With renewed strength, George ran for the car. He threw his arms out and latched onto Dana's hand, pulling himself up. Before he could get all the way inside, his foot slipped and he dropped. Dana held tight.

Struggling, George's strength left him rapidly. His feet dangled from the train, brushing the tracks below. As the train picked up speed, fear filled Dana.

"George," she said looking right into his eyes.

George stared back at her and she knew what he planned.

"Let me go," he said.

Dana shook her head. "No."

George slipped again, nearly taking Dana with him. Her sweaty hands made clinging to him difficult, but she refused to let go.

"I forgive you."

"George, please."

"Live for the both of us," said George.

"No," Dana said through tears.

"I'm sorry."

George used his one free hand to wrench himself out of Dana's grasp before they both fell. His body slammed into the dirt with a sickening crunch. Dana watched with horror as his body flipped over several times before coming to a stop.

"GEORGE!"

She watched helplessly as Colonel Fernau and his officers reached George's still form. He said something, but she didn't hear it over the roar of the wind. A single gunshot rang out, telling her that her friend was dead.

Dana stared out at the passing earth. The thought of jumping out raced through her mind. She put her hands on the sides of the doorway and prepared to leap, but stopped. George's words echoed through her head.

Live for the both of us.

With tears spilling from her eyes, Dana crawled to the back of the empty car. She hugged her knees, staring out the open door and feeling utterly alone.

Get the entire Dystopia Trilogy

Dystopia (Book 1)
Tempered Steel (Book 2)
Liberty's Torch (Book 3)

Imagine living in a world where everything you do is controlled.

Dana Ginary lives in a world where every aspect of her life is controlled by the Dystopian Government. Forced to work in Waste Management, her life becomes a nightmare with hunger and survival is her only constant. Before she knows it, she is caught up in a resistance movement and exiled from Dystopia, forced to find her way in the barren wastelands. While there, she must learn to live independently and discover how far she is willing to go to live and achieve freedom.

Also available on audio.

About the Author

Janet McNulty began her writing career with the Legends Lost series, published under the name of Nova Rose.

Ms. McNulty began the Dystopia Trilogy over a year ago with an idea she had carried with her since high school. A fan of books such as *Animal Farm, 1984, and Brave New World* she decided to create her own vision of a world gone terribly wrong.

More by Janet McNulty

The Mellow Summers Series

Sugar And Spice And Not So Nice
Frogs, Snails, And A Lot Of Wails
An Apple A Day Keeps Murder Away
Three Little Ghosts
Oh Holy Ghost
Where Trouble Roams
Two Ghosts Haunt A Grove
Trick Or Treat Or Murder
Roses Are Red…He's Dead
Double, Double Nothing But Trouble
Ring Around The Rosy, Not Another Ghosty

Mellow Summers moves to Vermont to attend college, accompanied by her friend Jackie. They soon find themselves running into ghosts and one mystery after another.

The Solaris Saga

Each novel has a companion coloring book.

Solaris Seethes
Solaris Seeks
Solaris Strays
Solaris Soars

Every myth has a beginning

After escaping the destruction of her home planet, Lanyr, with the help of the mysterious Solaris, Rynah must put her faith in an ancient legend. Never one to believe in stories and legends, she is forced to follow the ancient tales of her people: tales that also seem to predict her current situation.

Forced to unite with four unlikely heroes from an unknown planet (the philosopher, the warrior, the lover, the inventor) in order to save the Lanyran people, Rynah and Solaris embark on an adventure that will shatter everything Rynah once believed.

Also available on audio.

The Legends Lost Series

Published under Nova Rose

Tesnayr
Amborese
Galdin

Enter the Lands of Tesnayr and join on an epic fantasy adventure that spans over 1,500 years.

Begin with Tesnayr, the first king of the five lands as he unites the against a savage foe bent on their destruction.

Next, Join Amborese as she fights reclaim the throne after her family was forced to flee from it.

Thinking peace has finally entered the land, follow Galdin as he returns to Tesnayr to find it greatly hanged. Barbarians, led by a mysterious sorcerer, burn and destroy as they go. And only Galdin can stop them if he chooses to accept his fate.

Grandpa's Stories

My grandfather grew up in Arizona during the 1920s and 1930s. One week after the attack on Pearl Harbor he joined the Navy. During the summer of 2012, my mother visited him and recorded his stories about growing up, World War II, and his time as an employee at the Pacific Bell Telephone Company. This is the history of the 20th century as he lived it. These recordings make up this book. These are his words.

Something for the Little Ones

The Dragon Who series

The Dragon Who was Afraid of the Dark
The Dragon Who Went to the Moon
The Dragon Who Found a Monster Party
The Dragon Who Found a Spider in His Shoe
The Dragon Who Explored the Sea
The Dragon Who Caught a Cold

The Fairy Who series

The Fairy Who Lost a Tooth
The Fairy Who Got Lost

The Mr. Chili series

Mr. Chili's Chili
Mr. Chili Goes To School
Mr. Chili's Halloween
Mr. Chili's Christmas

Others:

Mrs. Duck and the Dragon
The Hungry Washing Machine
Rhymes-a-lot
Are You the Monster Under My Bed?
How Do You Catch An Alien

www.ingramcontent.com/pod-product-compliance
Lightning Source LLC
Chambersburg PA
CBHW032003240626

47153CB00003B/1099